Volume Four

AIRSHIP 27 PRODUCTIONS

Sinbad: The New Voyages Volume 4
Sinbad and the Golden Fleece © 2014 Joe Bonadonna
Sinbad and the Scorpion God © 2014 Ralph L. Angelo Jr.
Sinbad and the Isle of Madness © 2014 Jeff "Venture" Fournier
Sinbad and the Rakshasa's Game © 2014 I.A. Watson

Published by Airship 27 Productions
www.airship27.com
www.airship27hangar.com

Interior illustrations © 2014 Phil Cho
Cover illustration © 2014 Pat Carbajal

Editor: Ron Fortier
Associate Editor: Gordon Dymowski
Production and design: Rob Davis
Marketing and Promotions: Michael Vance

ISBN-13: 978-0692336038 (Airship 27)
ISBN-10: 0692336036

1 2 3 4 5 6 7 8 9 0

Volume Four
TABLE OF CONTENTS

SINBAD AND THE GOLDEN FLEECE

by Joe Bonadonna

S tanding before the black, stone altar, Sinbad El Ari wiped sweat from his mahogany-colored face. Ordinarily, small, enclosed places did not bother him. This chamber, however, set deep inside the bowels of a castle that had fallen into ruin eons ago, happened to be an altogether different matter. It was too small for his liking. The reek of long-dead things was an aroma he didn't much care for, either.

He glanced back at the way he had come, down the long, narrow tunnel that led directly to this chamber. Fresh air and bright sunlight beckoned from the mouth of the cave to which he had climbed, scaling the side of the cliff using rope and grappling hook; it was the only entrance to the chamber that he could find. A pair of stalagmites jutting from the stone floor of the cave held the grappling hook between them, from which hung his rope.

Disappointed that he did not find what he and his crew had sailed to Africa in search of, Sinbad turned back to face the altar. Squatting toad-like on the opposite side of the altar, a large stone statue of a fish-faced devil with a man's body stared back at him. Sinbad expected the statue to come to life as he reached for the single blue rose that, apparently, had been set upon the altar as an offering, ages ago. What was even more astonishing than the color of the rose was that, although faded and withered with age, it still remained whole.

Securing the blue rose inside his shirt, Sinbad heard the crack of stone breaking apart. He looked up just as the statue's hands broke free and dropped to the floor behind the altar. Next, the statue's yellow eyes popped out of their sockets and fell to the floor. Then the mouth grated open and a monstrous frog the size of a horse slithered out, landed on the altar and began croaking at Sinbad. Slowly drawing his scimitar, he backed away from the altar. But the creature did not attack. It just squatted there, baring and licking its fangs.

A moment later, the two hands crawled out from behind and either side of the altar.

"Allah's Beard!" he cried.

No longer made of stone but of fish-belly white flesh, the hands had grown to the size of hunting dogs. Each hand walked on thumb and three fingers that resembled the legs of the rhinoceros. The middle fingers had turned into monstrous cobras with long, forked tongues.

Weighing the odds, and with common sense winning out over valor, Sinbad turned and ran back down the tunnel and toward the cave opening.

The ruins of the ancient castle perched like a broken crown atop the cliff of a small island rising high above the waters of the inland lake. A narrow river wound its way like a drunken snake, disappeared around a bend and led to the south-eastern coast of Africa. It was a pure, idyllic setting. Reflected in the mirrored surface of the peaceful lake, the sunlight was almost blinding. Birds sang and monkeys chattered in the forest main-land surrounding the lake.

A cave, cut into the side of the island's cliff just below the castle ruins, gaped like the near-toothless mouth of an aging ogre. Hanging from a grappling hook wedged between two fang-like stalagmites was a length of rope, the end of which dangled beside a longboat.

Waiting patiently in the boat were Ralf Gunarson, Henri Delacrois and Tishimi Osara. They shaded their eyes with their hands as they stared at the cave, the only known ingress and egress to the ancient castle. Henri leaned on his bow, mumbling and cursing to himself in French. Ralf scratched his yellow beard and chewed on a fingernail. Tishimi sat in the stern, quiet and composed as she manned the tiller.

"By Odin, Henri!" Ralf growled. "Your lust for gold will be the death of you!"

Henri plucked his bowstring. "And you, my friend, your lack of fear will sooner see you in Hell than in your cherished Valhalla."

"The captain is mad. You know that, don't you?"

"This I know. So what is your point?"

"I'll wager he doesn't find any gold. You're a gambling man. What say you to a little wager, little man? I say he doesn't find any gold."

"I would not care to put the jinx on him." Henri stroked his thick brown mustache. "But I *will* make the bet on something else."

While they discussed their wager, Tishimi Osara adjusted her *daisho,* her long and short swords, and shook her head. "Men," she mumbled with disgust. Then she caught sight of something emerging from the cave. "Stand alert, boys!" she shouted, pointing to the cave.

"What's that?" asked Ralf.

"Bats," she replied. "Henri, I think you should nock an arrow to your bow."

The soles of Sinbad's sandals crunched old bones strewn about the floor of the tunnel. A swarm of bats almost knocked him over as they flew past him and escaped through the mouth of the cave. Tentacles with clawed hands emerged from the stone walls on either side of him, groping for him as he dashed past them. Crawling after him like a pair of monstrous scarabs, the hand-creatures closed in as he raced toward daylight, their wicked tongues whipping and lashing, coming ever closer. Behind him, the croaking of the giant frog echoed throughout the tunnel.

As luck would have it, one of Sinbad's sandal straps chose that moment to break. The sandal came loose. Sinbad stumbled just as he reached the lip of the cave. Demonic tongues wrapped around his legs the same instant he fell head-first out of the cave. An eye's blink before he slammed into the side of the cliff, he managed to twist his body to one side and make a grab for the rope. Instead of his face kissing the face of the cliff, his left hip crashed into it. Not only did the jar loosen his grip on his sword, he failed to seize the rope. Dazed and bruised, he felt himself being hauled upward by the tongues of the hand-things.

Something whistled past his head at that moment, and then he heard one of the creatures hiss loudly. Then the tongue wrapped around his left leg loosened its hold on him. Dangling in the air, he tried to grab the rope again, but he was swaying back and forth too much, and he was getting dizzy from the blood rushing to his brain. When he looked below him, he could see Henri nocking another arrow to his bow. Sinbad felt himself hauled up right to the bottom lip of the cave mouth just as another arrow *whooshed* past his ear. Another serpent-like hiss sounded. Then his right leg came free.

"Praise Allah!" he shouted as he dropped into the lake below.

A moment later, the monstrous frog dived into the water.

"Did I not tell you that the Capitaine would miss the boat?" Henri asked Ralf after the huge Viking handed him three dinars.

"Fools!" said Tishimi, rising to her feet. She drew her *tanto,* her short blade, and then unsheathed the *katana;* the longsword containing the soul of her father. "Draw steel!"

No sooner were the words out of her mouth when the demonic frog reached the side of the boat and lunged toward Ralf and Henri, causing them to tumble over the side of the boat.

As the monster attempted to climb into the boat, Tishimi raced toward it like a divine wind. Her *katana* sliced off the top of the thing's head, and then she stabbed one of its eyes with the *tanto.* The monster croaked in agony, but managed to get partway into the boat. Then Ralf and Henri bobbed to the surface of the lake. Henri pulled from his quiver the only arrow not lost in the lake, and rammed the frog in the back of the head with it. Tishimi cut and stabbed at it again, which gave Ralf time to climb into the boat, unsling his great battle axe and split the frog's head in two. Spurting black and green blood, the monster slid back into the lake and sank below its dark water.

Ralf helped Henri back into the boat. *"Merci, mon ami."*

"Now where the devil's Sinbad?" asked Ralf.

"Here I am!" Sinbad called, swimming toward them.

"Where have you been?" Henri demanded as he and Ralf helped Sinbad into the boat.

"At the bottom of the lake, looking for my sword," Sinbad told him, grinning and holding aloft his Persian sword.

Tishimi bowed to him. *"Konnichi wa!"*

Sinbad grinned and bowed in return.

"Did you not find that ram's head or whatever it is?" Henri asked Sinbad.

Sinbad shook his head, spraying water in the air. "It's a fleece, Henri. A golden fleece."

"But you did not find it?"

"I'm afraid not."

"Your princess will be most disappointed, Sinbad," said Tishimi.

"Then what *did* you find?" Ralf asked, wiping water from his face.

"This!" Sinbad removed the blue rose, now wet and limp but still in one piece, from inside his shirt.

"This...this is what you find...a *rose?*" asked Henri.

"But it's a *blue* rose," said Sinbad.

"The only color that has any value to me is gold!"

Rolling her eyes, Tishimi returned to her place at the tiller, where she sat and cleaned her swords. She bowed her head to the blade of her *katana*. "Oh, Father. Once again I ask you to give me strength to deal with these boys," she whispered.

While the men continued to argue amongst themselves, Tishimi heard what sounded to her ears like the rattling of old bones. She glanced up at the cave in the side of the cliff.

"Gentlemen, we are about to entertain more guests," she said, pointing.

Having each sprouted four hairy and skeleton-thin black legs, gaping maws with rows of serrated teeth, and huge, clacking mandibles; the two yellow eyes of the monstrous statue crawled down the side of the cliff like great spiders out to trap four human flies.

Ralf groaned and took his place at the oars. "By Thor's Hammer! Let's be gone from here. I'd like to make it back to the Blue Nymph while there's light enough to drink by!"

"You lost a sandal, Capitaine," Henri pointed out.

Sinbad looked down at his one bare foot. "So I have."

Many months later, following a long and uneventful voyage home, Sinbad and white-bearded Rafi, shipmate, scholar, and student of Greek medicine, stood in the presence of Haroun al-Rashid, Defender of the Faith and Caliph of all Baghdad.

Sinbad eyed the humpbacked dwarf standing next to the Caliph; Prince Amahd, a distant relative of the Caliph's. The man was known to have contacts and dealings with the underworld of Baghdad, which often proved embarrassing to the Caliph. With them were an elderly gray-haired man and a beautiful young woman with dark eyes and hair.

"Twice now you have failed in your quest to attain for me the Golden Fleece of ancient Greek legend," the Caliph said to Sinbad. "I am very disappointed in you, you know."

"A thousand pardons, O Light of Islam," Sinbad replied. "In all truth, it seems that no matter where we sail, no matter where we search, the Fleece remains ever elusive."

The Caliph turned and conferred in barely-audible whispers with Amahd and his other two guests. Sinbad cast a glance at Rafi, who shrugged.

"Politics," said he.

Sinbad laughed softly and looked around the chamber in which they were gathered. It was not the throne room, but a lavishly-appointed trophy chamber where al-Rashid stored his vast collection of rare toys and paintings, sculptures, books, a clockwork owl and horse, a mechanical minotaur, and various ancient relics and artifacts from across the known world; many of which Sinbad and his crew had brought back from their voyages.

While Rafi's eyes glittered with amazement at sight of such splendiferous artifacts, Sinbad had eyes only for the young woman in the crimson sari. Boldly she stood in the presence of the Caliph, face unveiled, head uncovered. Her eyes, black as a night sky, sparkled with a purplish light that was ethereal and intoxicating. Just as black was her mane of flowing hair, while her lips, drawn in a ghost of a smile, were lush and as red as the blood of the grape. Sinbad's heart galloped like an Arabian stallion.

Rafi elbowed Sinbad in the ribs. "Have you forgotten the Princess Yasmina so soon?" he asked, nodding toward the balcony that overlooked the chamber at the far end of the room.

Managing to steer his attention away from the black-haired woman, Sinbad looked up and saw the Princess Yasmina, the Caliph's cousin, watching him from the balcony. Veiled modestly and wearing a blue, diaphanous dress, she was accompanied by two elderly women.

Sinbad's blood now stirred hotter than a potion boiling in a witch's cauldron. He blew a kiss to the princess and bowed to her in a most overly theatrical manner. Her dark eyes flashed, she returned a brief nod, and then drifted away through a door with her attendants close behind.

"The head never rules a fickle heart, but just becomes its partner in crime," said Rafi.

"Ah, but all great discoveries are made by men whose feelings run ahead of their thinking," Sinbad replied.

The Caliph coughed loudly to gain Sinbad's attention. "My dear Captain, it is most propitious that you should return to me on this very day."

"How so, O Star of Heaven?" asked Sinbad.

"My guests have travelled here to Baghdad from the kingdom of Videha, in India. I present to you the scholar, Bharat Hassan."

The color of the grey-haired man's plain, brown robe was almost as dark as his eyes. "I am so much honored to meet the most illustrious Captain Sinbad El Sari," he stated. He bowed at the waist and motioned with his hand toward the young woman. "And this is my daughter, Urmila, who is herself a most accomplished and respected scholar."

Sinbad had never heard of Videha; there were still places in the world even he had not yet visited. "Welcome to Baghdad," he said with an even more flamboyant bow.

"Greetings to you, Captain Sinbad," Urmila spoke in a sweet and musical voice.

"The honor is all mine, fair lady," he said.

"Now," spoke the Caliph. "My guests have a proposition for you, Sinbad."

"My ears are yours, Your Greatness."

Bharat stroked his short, gray beard, and then from inside his robe he brought forth a rolled up sheet of papyrus. "The Caliph's search for the Golden Fleece has long been of most interest to me. It parallels my own search for another artifact from ancient Greece."

"Pandora's Box," Urmila explained.

Sinbad now found this meeting to be almost as tantalizing as Urmila's smile. "What need have you for that fabled box, if I may ask?"

Bharat cleared his throat. "The people of Videha have suffered a witch's curse; a foul spell uttered from her lips before the flames of the pyre consumed her flesh."

"The Curse of Despair," said Urmila. "Our people are ill and dying of hopelessness."

Sinbad knew the story of Pandora's Box, of course. However, as with the Golden Fleece, he had his doubts concerning its existence.

"But Pandora's Box has been lost for ages, far longer than even the Fleece has been lost," said Rafi. "I have studied its history. No one knows what happened to it."

"We believe we have discovered its whereabouts," said Bharat. "And we believe that it is hidden in the same location where the Golden Fleece may be found."

Bharat went on to explain how his life had been dedicated to finding the lost artifacts of Greece, such as the inventions of Daedalus. He believed they had all been stolen and hidden away by Medea of Colchis, the first wife of Jason of Thessaly.

"In a jealous rage after Jason set her aside and married the Princess of Corinth, believing herself betrayed by the gods, Medea conjured a great magic, stole those precious relics and hid them from the eyes of both Man and Gods," said Urmila.

"And you seek my help, and that of my ship and crew," stated Sinbad.

Bharat handed him the map. "My research has uncovered an island lying beyond the Pillars of Heracles, an island hidden by white mist and surrounded by a great barrier reef."

Sinbad unrolled the map and studied it. "The Pillars of Heracles?"

"The Iberian Emirate of Cordoba," Rafi explained.

"Remember our bargain, Sinbad," said the Caliph. "If you wish to marry my cousin Yasmina, you must find and bring to me the Golden Fleece. And *this*, I might add, is your third and last chance. Fail me, and I give her hand in marriage to the Sultan of Oman."

How could I forget? Sinbad asked himself. In a moment of weakness, he had agreed to the Caliph's terms. Thus, there was but one answer he could give.

"I hear and I obey, O Sun that shines over Baghdad. I am yours to command, my Caliph."

"Excellent! Most excellent!"

Sinbad studied the map again. "Such a journey will prove arduous, at best, Your Grace, and we would not return for at least a year; if we return at all."

"And if I may ask, Great Caliph," said Rafi. "If this island is enshrouded in white mist and surrounded by a barrier reef, how do we find it? How do we reach its shores?"

"Amahd is my third cousin, twice removed, and he has the solution to that problem." The Caliph turned to Amahd. "Cousin, you may speak."

The dwarf with the humpback bowed to his royal relative and spoke up for the first time. "I have discussed this matter with Galgo al-Jamel," he said. "Is his name familiar to you?"

"A magicman of some kind, I believe," said Rafi.

"Indeed," said Amahd. "He can get us there, ship and crew, inside of three days."

"But there is no canal or river that can take the Blue Nymph to the waters of the Mediterranean is such a short time," said Sinbad.

"We shall need neither wind nor water, Captain."

"Then how do we reach this island? Do we fly like the crow?"

Amahd rubbed his hands together. "You must learn to place your trust in the brother of the woman you wish to marry, Sinbad."

Pinned to the black velvet of the night sky, the crescent moon, the Moon of Islam, burned cold and bright like the all-seeing, all-knowing eye of Allah, the Great and Compassionate.

Sinbad, Tishimi, and Amahd strolled through the dark heart of Moga Alley. Beggars, the halt and the lame, the blind and the sick, all walked or crawled over those wet and slime-ridden cobblestones. Even though many were undoubtedly thieves, cutthroats and charlatans, Sinbad nonetheless paved the way with gold, for these were his people, and he would often do what he could to ease their burdens. He would not have it said that an El Sari had turned a cold shoulder to the poor, the elderly and the helpless of Baghdad.

Beside him, Tishimi walked as silently as a cat stalking a mouse, hands on the hilts of her two weapons. Sinbad trusted her without question and had nothing but the highest respect for her. She was a loyal and trusted shipmate, comrade, and above all, friend.

"Why are you so eager to help us, Amahd?" asked Sinbad. It was something of a miracle and a mystery to him how a husband and wife could create a daughter as beauteous as the Princess Yasmina, and then produce her unfortunately misshapen brother.

"The Caliph has promised to find me a wife, in return for my helping his most illustrious and favored of all subjects," replied the dwarf prince.

"Are you sure you know the way, Amahd?" asked Tishimi.

"Not much farther, my dear," said he. "Ah . . . here it is!"

They had come to the end of the alley, where stood a wall of black stone. A single door stood in the center of this wall; there were no windows. Amahd knocked at the door. In the distance, hounds wailed and howled at the crescent moon.

When the door opened, a thin and wizened man opened and bid them enter. He had a shaved head, a sweeping mustache, and wore the desert garb of a Bedouin.

"Greetings, Amahd," he said. "So, this must be Captain Sinbad and the lovely Tishimi Osara. I am Galgo al-Jamel. Welcome, be welcome. Come in and sit. I have tea."

The magicman stepped aside to welcome his guests into his parlor. Sinbad was last to enter, and as the door closed behind him he saw shadows flitting back and forth at the far end of the alley. *Stray dogs, no doubt,* he told himself.

Inside, it was the usual abode of a wizard, filled with all the tools of the trade: crucibles, alembics, beakers, mortars and pestles, books and scrolls, and even a cauldron bubbling in a small hearth. The place was quite clean and quite homey, however. Galgo bid his guests to be seated at the large table in the center of the room, and then he poured them each a cup of tea.

"So, Amahd tells me you seek the Golden Fleece," he said directly to Sinbad.

"Indeed," said the captain, seeing no need to say more than was necessary. He brought out the map, unrolled and spread it out upon the table.

"I have never seen a map that extends so far west of the Iberian Peninsula," said the magicman. "And this strange island marked here. What is it called?"

"It has no name, so far as I know," said Sinbad.

Amahd studied the map. "Why, that's close to the edge of the world!"

"I hold to the theory that the earth is round," said Sinbad. "One day I shall prove it, too."

"Now that is quite preposterous," Amahd scoffed.

"Mind your manners in my home, Prince Amahd. I happen to agree with Sinbad," said Galgo. He turned to Sinbad. "Where did you acquire this map?"

"From a scholar named Bharat Hassan, of Videha."

"A wise and learned man, I have heard." Galgo pored over the map for another moment. "Have you sailed the Mediterranean in search of the Fleece?"

"Not as yet," said Sinbad. "We've sailed the Indian Ocean and the Arabian Sea, down through Madagascar and the land of the Hottentots, and even to the distant land of the Australoids. But we have yet to strike for the waters of the Mediterranean. Such a voyage requires much planning, as we would be gone for well over a year."

"Amahd claims you can guide us to this island in the space of three days," said Tishimi.

"Indeed, I can," said Galgo, "for a price, of course."

Outside, the hounds continued to howl, now louder and closer.

"Where did you acquire this map?"

"And what is your price?" asked Sinbad.

Galgo al-Jamel held out a hand and rubbed thumb and two fingers together. "An equal share of whatever…"

The magicman's words were cut short when something huge and powerful began pounding against the locked door.

They were all on their feet in an instant. Sinbad and Tishimi stood with hands on sword hilts as they turned and faced the entrance. Amahd cowered in a corner, near a shelf containing glass beakers. Galgo stood his ground, unarmed and unafraid.

Of a sudden the door crashed open and four creatures stormed into the home of the magicman. They resembled hunting dogs, but their hides were scaly, like the skin of the lizard. Four legs and clawed feet they had, and two arms and hands, with three talons on each. Their faces were a blasphemous hybrid of man and dog and serpent, with bright yellow eyes.

"What in the name of the Prophet are these things?" cried Amahd.

In unison, Sinbad and Tishimi drew their swords.

"*Canisaurs*, I think," said Galgo, searching for something on a small table behind him.

The first of the monsters attacked.

Sinbad sprang forward to take on the canisaur. Like a cobra forged of Persian steel, his sword hissed as it lashed out and sliced open the belly of the reptilian dog. The creature fell to its knees but lashed out with its talons before it toppled over. Sinbad hopped out of the way just in time, and then buried his sword in its skull for good measure. He wrenched free his weapon and spun around to carve in half the snout of a second fiend. Drops of dark red blood sprinkled the air as the canisaur fell dead at his feet. Turning swiftly, he saw that Amahd and Galgo were squeezed into a corner as two more of the monsters pressed forward. Kicking over the table to throw an obstacle in the path of the creatures, he rushed to help the men, hacking and slashing all about him. Two more canisaurs then stormed into the house.

Tishimi ducked a swipe from a razor-clawed hand that might have taken her scalp, had she not been so quick to move. Her *katana* whistled in the air and sheared clean through the neck of one canisaur. Its head sailed across the room, trailing drops of blood, crashed into a wall, and dropped to the floor. The monster's corpse fell over. The jaws of another fiend snapped too close to her for comfort. Cursing in her native tongue, she stumbled backward, but managed to use her short sword to slice the canisaur's throat. When the creature dropped to its knees she punctured its heart with one powerful thrust of her *katana*. Then she leapt over the table and rushed to help Sinbad protect Amahd and Galgo.

Another pair of canisaurs barged into the house of the magicman. One of them threw itself upon Sinbad, and they tumbled to the floor. Tishimi's *tanto* stabbed one canisaur straight between its all-too human eyes, and then plunged her sword in the spine of the monster on top of Sinbad. She kicked the carcass aside and helped him to his feet. He smiled and bowed to her.

Still another canisaur charged through the doorway.

"Duck!" he told Tishimi.

When she tucked in her head and stooped low, Sinbad's curved blade whistled in the air above her and sheared off the top of the canisaur's skull.

"Arigato!" she said.

Five more reptilian hounds forced their way into the house.

Amahd cried out in pain and fell against the shelf when one of the beasts clawed his arm. The shelf toppled over with a sound of breaking glass, showering the dwarf with shards and splinters. At that moment, Galgo found what he was looking for, a jar containing tiny white crystals, and he threw a handful into the monster's face. The canisaur howled and whined in pain. It backed away, wiping its eyes with the knuckles of its hands.

"There's too many of them!" Amahd screamed.

Sinbad stabbed the fiend through the back of the skull. "Nonsense!" he shouted.

Tishimi joined him, and their swords composed a song of steel and death.

Galgo stepped forward, holding the jar in both hands. "Stand aside!" he yelled. Then he threw the contents of the jar into the air, and it was like a fall of snow inside his home.

When the white granules fell upon the canisaurs, the devils began to hiss and wail, their reptilian flesh and human-like faces now burning, their eyes blinded. Taking advantage of the situation, Sinbad and Tishimi leapt into the middle of the canisaur pack and set to with sharp steel, cleaving and slicing as if they were a pair of butchers. Blood splattered the room. The bodies of the reptilian dogs piled up. Howls soon turned into whim-pers, which soon turned into silence. When it was over, Galgo's house resembled an abattoir.

"Anyone hurt?" asked Sinbad.

Tishimi and Galgo shook their heads, but Amahd showed the captain his arm. It bled from a trio of nasty scratches across his forearm.

"I guess I am," he said.

Galgo studied the dwarf's arm. "You'll live. We'll get this bandaged before we leave."

"What manner of magic powder did you use, Galgo?" asked Tishimi.

"Oh, there was no magic in that," he told her. "It was just ordinary salt. Demons have no tolerance for it. Works every time."

"Where did those devils come from and why did they attack?" asked Sinbad.

"They were the pets of a rival sorcerer from whom I stole the secret of how to transform a sea-going vessel into one that sails through the air."

"You can make the Blue Nymph fly?"

"Of course. I *am* a wizard, you know."

"Where is this foe of yours now?" asked Tishimi.

Galgo held up a finger, then turned and reached for a leather sack lying on the floor in one corner. Reaching inside it, he pulled out the near-mummified head of a man.

"I did not think his Hellhounds would track me down," he explained, tossing the head onto the pile of dead canisaurs. "It was a fair fight."

He walked over to where lay the head of the first canisaur Tishimi had slain, picked it up and stuffed it inside the leather sack.

"What are you going to do with that?" asked Sinbad.

Galgo winked and tapped the side of his nose with a finger. "The heads of demons are very valuable and possess certain magical properties."

The wind blew cool and refreshing in Sinbad's face as he stood on the forecastle deck of the Blue Nymph. The air was thin, too, at this great height. Quiet and serene, so close to Heaven, the great ship sailed directly below the clouds. Far below, the blue waters of the Mediterranean Sea sparkled and mirrored the light from the sun. High above, dipping in and out of the clouds, were a number of strange-looking birds.

Three days earlier, Sinbad and his crew had left Basra to the cheers and astonishment of the crowds that had assembled to watch the Blue Nymph take flight.

Standing on deck next to Sinbad, Rafi seemed in his glory, as if he'd been born to fly. He breathed in a great lungful of cool air and then exhaled, slowly.

"Beautiful, are they not, the *peris*?" he asked.

"Indeed they are," Sinbad agreed. "Galgo is a magicman of the highest degree, to have the power and knowledge to summon such creatures to do his bidding."

"Keep in mind, he stole the secret from another mage. Murdered him, too."

"Such is the way with wizards. They are scoundrels. So are we, in one way or another."

Sinbad marveled at the wondrous creatures carrying the Blue Nymph on her voyage through the clouds and toward the Isle of the Golden Fleece.

Seven of the *peris*, there were: three to port, three to starboard, and one forward; roughly twenty or so feet from the ship. Each *peri* was taller and stronger than the Cyclops that had tried to roast and eat Sinbad and his crew on the Isle of Colossa. The bodies of the *peris* shimmered as if composed of fire and light; crimson and gold, and silver and white in color. They had massive wings of black feathers that flapped gently and gracefully against the wind.

Attached to, and hanging from, the manacles that shackled the wrists of these ethereal beings were chains of blue steel. The ends of the chains were secured to the ship's hull, rails and prow, allowing the *peris* to carry and guide the Blue Nymph through the air. On occasion, the ship would sway from side to side as if she were being rocked on the bosom of a gentle sea. The *peris* never slept, never ate. They were tireless and relentless, and obedient in their servitude. Save for the soothing song they hummed in total harmony, the beings flew in relative silence, mindful of their task, yet paying no attention to the crew of the ship they carried.

"The *peris* are the descendants of fallen angels, born in Hell," Rafi explained. "The chains they bear are the sins of their forebears."

"The sins of the fathers, visited upon the sons," Sinbad remarked.

"Indeed, though the *peris* are innocent of sin and crime. Allah, in his infinite mercy, will grant them Heaven one day, after they serve his purpose here on earth."

"You are quite the scholar, my friend."

Rafi bowed to his captain. "Now I will play ship's doctor and see how our men fare. Sea legs they may have, but some have no stomach for this."

Turning from the rail, Rafi went down to see to the men.

Sinbad looked upon his crew with pride, each having volunteered for this voyage. Only Tishimi and his three passengers were not on deck. Galgo the magicman had returned to the guest cabin he shared with Bharat the scholar, after breaking his morning fast. Tishimi was also in her cabin, which she had reluctantly agreed to share with Urmila. As for Bharat Hassan and his daughter Urmila, Sinbad had not seen them since they retired after dinner the night before.

The Blue Nymph sailed the air with but a skeleton crew, for duties and chores the sailors would normally perform were not needed on this venture. The ship's wheel had been tied down, mast and rigging well secured, and sails furled and stored below. The crew had little to do but scrub decks, caulk where needed, and apply fresh paint to wherever Omar, the first mate, ordered them. He prowled the deck like a bulldog, growling and barking orders.

"Ajib, Badar, Jabbar! I want that deck cleaned and polished so I can use it as a shaving mirror!" he yelled at three of the newest hands.

The two young lads on hands and knees, with brushes and buckets, nodded and doubled their efforts. The third, holding a mop, began mopping away as if his life depended on it.

Haroun, the lookout, began climbing down from the crow's nest.

"Get back up there and keep those keen eyes peeled, you sea monkey!" Omar shouted.

"But there's naught to see except the clouds!" said Haroun.

"Then you'll be the first to know when it starts to rain!"

Shaking his head, Haroun scrambled back up the mast to take his place in the nest.

Ralf, Henri and Amahd were leaning over the starboard rail.

"And just what do you three sluggards think you're doing?" Omar demanded.

"Spitting contest!" the big Viking yelled over a shoulder.

Henri turned, wiped his mouth, and grinned. "I am enjoying the most marvelous view!"

His face deathly-white, Amahd turned from the rail and plopped down on the wooden crate upon which he had been standing. He had begged Sinbad to take him along on the voyage, but Sinbad had stood firm against it. The Caliph then intervened on Amahd's behalf and reminded Sinbad that the ne'er-do-well Prince was soon to become his brother thru marriage… *if* the Golden Fleece was found, that is. Now the humpbacked dwarf was sorry he had come along. His arm, still bandaged, he often used as an excuse to shirk his duties. But he did look quite ill, even feverish. In spite of that, he found the strength to summon a grim smile.

"And I am feeding the fish," he said.

Then he gagged and vomited all over the deck.

"Grab a mop and clean that up, you crook-back imp!" shouted Omar.

"But I am a Prince, and the Caliph's cousin!" Amahd protested.

"*Third* cousin," said Henri.

"Twice removed," Ralf reminded him.

"Clean up your mess or I'll feed *you* to the fish!" Sinbad yelled at Amahd.

Far above the Blue Nymph, wheeling in and out of the clouds, three large birds circled the air as if they were following the ship. They screeched and cawed, but the wind quickly carried away their cries. Sinbad was about to use his spyglass for a closer look when they suddenly disappeared in a thick bank of clouds.

"A glorious day to be alive, is it not, Captain?"

Sinbad turned as Urmila came toward him. He had not heard her footsteps, so silent had been the approach of this beauty from India.

Urmila was as mysterious as the land of her birth. Her black eyes glowed with that violet light, a light that did not emanate from this world. Her body moved and swayed like a dancer's, her voice echoed with undertones of heavenly music, and her smile had the power to stop a man's heart. Ordinarily, Sinbad would have flirted and romanced such a rare beauty as this woman, but there was something about her that had reined in his desire, something cold and distant. She was untouchable and unattainable . . . like a goddess of old.

"Indeed, it is," he said. "Are you comfortable, sharing quarters with Tishimi?"

"I am, but she doesn't seem too happy about it."

"What gives you reason to say that?"

"It's just a feeling, that's all. I don't think she trusts me."

"Tishimi is not one to give her trust and friendship lightly nor quickly."

"She is a most interesting woman, however. She was writing poetry, when I left her."

"She calls it *haiku*," Sinbad explained. "It is a form of verse common in her native land."

"Last night, I awoke from a dream and saw her polishing the blade of her sword."

"She is a swordswoman, Urmila. She cares for her weapons."

"But she was *whispering* to it, talking to it as if it were alive!"

Sinbad shrugged. "We all have our eccentricities."

The ship's tomcat, Samson, rubbed up against their legs. Urmila stooped and gathered the gray cat in her arms, scratching it behind the ears. Samson purred with contentment.

"He likes you," Sinbad said to her.

"I like cats." Urmila looked at the sky for a moment. "According to the map, we should spot the island late this afternoon."

"Perhaps this time we may actually find the cursed thing."

As if inspecting a new species of insect, Urmila studied Sinbad's face. "You still don't believe the Fleece exists, do you?"

"What I believe doesn't matter," he told her. "My Caliph believes it exists, and I believe in my Caliph. Above all things, I trust in Allah."

"But you leave your horse well hobbled."

"Camel, Urmila."

"I beg your pardon?"

"We tie up our camels."

"Oh!" She laughed softly, and then her manner grew thoughtful. "Princess Yasmina has truly captured your heart, to make you search the world for a thing you don't believe exists."

Caught off guard by her remark, Sinbad was at a loss for something to say. And then the screeching cries of those large birds echoed across the sky. Now the ship's crew was shielding their eyes as they pointed and stared at the sky. Sinbad set the spyglass to his eye, but the glimpse he caught of the creatures was fleeting, for once again they hid themselves in a thick expanse of white clouds. When he lowered the spyglass, Urmila bowed her head to him.

"Even though you don't believe in it, you *hope* the Golden Fleece exists," she said. "So you see, Sinbad, we both journey with hope in our hearts."

With that, Urmila Hassan kissed Samson on the nose, set him down, turned and went below. Samson scampered away to find a cozy place to nap.

The three large birds continued to follow the Blue Nymph all afternoon. Though they strayed in and out of the clouds, they never drew close to the ship. Their squawks and whistles echoed across the vault of Heaven. By now, the ship's crew had grown used to their company, and some hoped they would draw close enough to end up in the stewpot.

Henri and Ralf had finally recovered and began to enjoy sailing through the clouds. The big Viking reveled in the chilly wind, while the archer from Gaul mumbled, cursed and donned a second shirt. Amahd, on the other hand, was still quite ill. His face had gone even paler, but now there was a faint green hue to his pallor. Sweat dripped from his body, and his eyes were dull and lifeless. When he walked, his dizziness was apparent in every stumbling step he took.

"Go below before you befoul my nice clean deck again," Omar told him.

"But I am a prince as well as the Caliph's cousin and Sinbad is soon to marry my sister. You can't order me about like this!"

"I don't care if you are Ali Baba himself! Aboard the Blue Nymph, there are no princes or sultans, only sailors. And they all answer to me!"

Amahd fumbled for words but could not find any. So he gave the evil eye to Omar, spat over the ship's rail, and headed below.

Henri thumbed his bowstring and produced a low bass note as the dwarf stumbled past him. It was then that he noticed Badar, Jabbar and Ajib, gathered on the upper deck, watching the sky. Badar, with a small bow and arrow, was taking aim at the three strange birds wheeling about in the sky, high above the Blue Nymph. After a moment, Badar's bow hummed. The arrow shot straight into the air, reached the top of its arc, which was well below the intended targets, and began its descent. The wind had its way with the arrow as it fell to the sea far below.

Lounging against the rail, Samson yawned as he watched everyone with keen eyes.

Henri went over to join the three young sailors, followed by Ralf and Omar.

"Are you hoping to bring down our dinner?" Omar asked Badar.

Badar scratched his head. "I was trying. They are very much large enough to feed us all, and they may even taste good!"

"You will never succeed with such a pitiful bow as that," said Henri.

"Show the lad how it's done, O great archer!" Ralf said with a laugh.

Henri nocked a large arrow to his longbow, took careful aim at one of the great birds and let loose. The bowstring hummed as the bolt whistled in the air and took to the sky. There followed an ear-shivering screech as the first arrow scored. Not a moment later, Henri let fly a second arrow. Another angry, painful screech ripped across the sky. In the space of three quick heartbeats, the first bird tumbled from the sky, just off the port bow; an arrow in its heart.

"And that is how it is done, my friend," Henri said to the three lads.

The strange bird then fell onto one of the *peris* and passed completely *through* the huge offspring of a fallen angel as if it were made of smoke. The *peri* seemed oblivious to it all, never faltering, never distracted, its massive wings never missing a beat.

"By the Prophet!" Omar shouted in amazement.

A moment later, the second bird tumbled out of the sky with Henri's arrow in its breast. This one, however, landed with a crash on the main deck. A piercing screech ripped through the ears of the crew as the remaining bird took flight.

Samson the cat took off in silence, heading below as if a hunting dog were on his tail.

The crew gathered around the body of the fallen bird, startled and horrified, for it was not a bird at all, but something resembling a cross between a bat, a reptile, and a woman. It had large wings, dark blue flesh like the scales of a reptile, horns, fangs, a long tail, and sharp talons.

Henri crossed himself. *"Mon Dieu!"*

The rest of the crew stood still and silent, staring in wonder and fear at the creature. Rafi raced toward them, followed by Bharat and Urmila. Galgo the magicman joined them last, looking tired and weak, but still with a fire in his eyes.

"Hammer of Thor!" said Ralf. "That's no bird I've ever seen!"

Rafi studied the dead creature a moment. "It has the look of something ancient, something out of legend or myth."

"Gentlemen, we shall reach our destination before nightfall," said Bharat, stroking his short gray beard. "The map has led us true. This creature is proof of that."

"You don't trust Urmila, but you can't point a finger at any one reason why I shouldn't trust her, either," Sinbad said to Tishimi.

"Your head flounders, your fickle heart tumbles overboard, and your brain runs aground every time a pretty woman smiles at you," she told him.

Sinbad sipped the cup of green tea Tishimi had brewed, and sat with her at the small table in her cabin. Not one to socialize overly much with the crew, she could often be found in her cabin, where she would meditate, paint or write verse.

"Come now!" he said with a laugh. "There's little cause for jealousy."

Sinbad enjoyed teasing Tishimi, as she found pleasure in mocking him on occasion. He had nothing but the highest respect for her: she was a loyal and trusted shipmate, friend, and comrade in arms. Her opinion he held in the highest regard.

"And what of Princess Yasmina?" she asked. "You cannot love them both. Urmila is . . . she is not for you."

A solid thud sounded from above, as if something had fallen to the deck. Tishimi frowned, but Sinbad paid it no heed.

"I know," he said with a sigh of regret. "And I must admit that there *is* something in her manner. It's as if she has one foot in this world, and the other . . . elsewhere."

"Keep a close eye on her and Bharat. They have yet to reveal themselves, but I believe that before this voyage is done we will know what they are about. Whether for good or ill, I know in my heart that this journey will not turn out as we hope."

A smile stole its way across Sinbad's face. "Do they ever?"

An urgent pounding sounded at the cabin door, and then it swung open.

"Forgive this intrusion, Captain," said Omar. "But I think you should come on deck."

When Sinbad and Tishimi followed Omar to the upper deck, they found Urmila, Bharat, Galgo, and the Sindhi crew gathered around the corpse of the winged creature, pierced by one of Henri's long arrows.

"Merciful Allah...what a stench!" said Sinbad.

"*Mon Dieu!* I think this is a gorgon of the ancient times," said Henri.

"This is not one of Medusa's kin," said Bharat. "Else you'd have been turned to stone."

Rafi stood there with arms folded, staring at the creature. "This is a harpy, I believe."

"A cowardly breed, unless provoked," said Urmila.

"Do...do they eat men?" asked young Badar.

"Keep a close eye on her and Bharat."

"No, just their livers," said Urmila.

Haroun shouted down from the crow's next. "Captain, beware the sky!"

Sinbad and the others turned their eyes upon the afternoon sky, where the clouds were being swept away by a cold gust of wind.

A swarm of harpies dropped down out of the vanishing clouds, scores of them. Screeching and squawking like angry birds, they circled lower and lower towards the ship. There were many of them; far too many.

"Looks to me as if they've been well provoked," said Ralf, drawing his broadsword and massive double-bladed battle axe.

Sinbad glared at Henri. "Curse you, Henri!"

"I thought it was but a large bird!"

"Draw steel!" cried Tishimi, both her swords drawn and ready.

The harpies swooped down upon the Blue Nymph like the wrath of Allah.

Haroun started to climb down from the crow's nest. Then he screamed when a harpy seized his shoulders in its claws. Hanging onto the mast, he cried out for help.

An arrow tore its way through the neck of the harpy. The creature shrieked once, let go of Haroun, and dropped to the deck. Blood splashed the deck as its skull shattered apart.

"Get back up there and keep your head down!" Henri shouted to the look out.

Haroun scrambled up to the nest and hid himself from view.

As Henri was in the process of nocking another arrow to his bow, a harpy flew straight at him. But Ralf was there to skewer the fiend with his great broadsword. Then the giant Viking was grabbed from behind by another harpy, who struggled to lift him into the air. With one backward, over-the-head swing of his great axe, Ralf split the creature from belly to groin.

Jabbar tossed a belaying pin at a harpy, missed, and was seized by the monster. Ajib rushed to his aid with an old scimitar, fighting desperately to save his friend. But a second harpy slammed into him, knocked him to the deck and began tearing at him with its claws. Omar rushed in and tried to save both lads, his sword whistling with menace. He cut off the head of the harpy attacking Ajib, who crawled away to seek shelter. Omar then swung around, drops of blood flying from his blade. But it was too late: Jabbar's cries echoed in the air and diminished as he was carried aloft and away from the Blue Nymph.

The crew of the Blue Nymph was vastly outnumbered as more harpies dropped down out of the sky. Unfazed, the seven *peris* never faltered in their duty, did not even notice the battle raging aboard the decks of the Blue Nymph. And all the while, Bharat and Urmila stood calm and unmolested on the forecastle deck, to where they had retreated.

The swords of Sinbad and Tishimi glittered and whistled in the air as they hacked and hewed all around them, facing harpy after harpy and sending each down to ancient Hades. Galgo huddled against the main mast, guarded by those two great warriors.

Crewmen all around them were carried off by the harpies. The sailors were outnumbered at least three to one. Hard as the men fought, they could not win the day.

"Galgo!" Sinbad shouted. "Can you help? Can you conjure more magic?"

"I believe so, Captain!"

With that, the magicman took off running towards a hatch leading below.

"Henri, Ralf, cover Galgo's retreat!" Sinbad shouted.

The archer shot his arrows and the Viking set to all around him, sword and axe a deadly combination. Badar joined them, using sword and a ship's hammer like a gladiator of ancient Rome. Galgo made it safely to the companionway just as Amahd came on deck. He still looked sick, his face pale, and his eyes almost amber in color.

"What in Allah's name is…" he started to say.

"Get below!" Galgo interrupted. "When will you learn to follow orders, you fool?"

Amahd's ill-colored eyes flashed with anger at the magicman. But Galgo ignored the little humpback and hurried below.

When a harpy swooped down upon Amahd, he turned and raced toward the hatchway. Had one of Henri's arrows not skewered the fiend, Amahd would have gone to his doom.

Tishimi seemed to be everywhere at once. Cat-like and as graceful as a hareem dancer she was, slashing left and right with her swords. Not a harpy could touch her, so fast did she move, so deadly were her twin blades. Monstrous heads rolled. Blood stained the boards. Harpy corpses littered the deck. But then even she became hard-pressed as the devils from ancient times continued to plague the ship.

Sinbad stood with his back against the mast, his sword flashing in the sunlight, darting in and out like the tongue of the cobra. Harpies fell to that blade, unable to get to him. When he stepped away and raced to join Tishimi, he was overwhelmed. Fighting for his life, heart pounding, he ducked and stabbed, slashed and dodged aside. He slipped on blood, nearly fell, but managed to slice open the belly of one harpy before the claws of another raked his shoulder. Cursing the Devil, he spun around and felled the monster with a vicious stab to its belly. In that moment, four more harpies dived at him. He ducked and slew the first, and then the other three veered off, circled around and came at him again; one on his left, another on his right, the third angling straight down on him from above.

Then Tishimi was there at his side. Before Sinbad could slay the one on his right, the samurai's blades had cut the one on his left in half. Together their trio of swords neatly carved the third into three bloody pieces.

Sinbad bowed his thanks to Tishimi. She returned the gesture.

Galgo came back on deck a moment later, mumbling strange words and carrying the head of a woman with glowing yellow eyes and writhing serpents for locks of hair.

When he held aloft the head, the woman's eyes shot beams of burning, yellow light that lit up sky. The harpies shrieked in terror, caught in that blast of light, unable to look away. First one and then another turned to stone, then a third and a fourth. Down to the sea they fell, scores of the hell-born creatures. But many crashed to the decks of the Blue Nymph, breaking apart like ancient mud bricks. Torsos, arms, legs, heads, and wings shattered into hundreds of pieces. Men scattered out of the way as bodies that had once been flesh showered them with chips and chunks of stone, grit and dust. Many were hit by flying, sharp-edged debris. By the Mercy of Allah, none were seriously injured, though most suffered cuts, scratches and bruises.

And then, before the sky was cleared of harpies, fatigue caused Galgo to drop the gorgon's head. His shoulders sagged with exhaustion when a harpy swooped down upon him. A pair of talons ripped into his shoulders. The magicman screamed and dropped the head.

Before he could be carried from the ship, Tishimi leapt into the air with feet aimed for the harpy's head. The fiend shrieked as its face exploded with blood, and finally it let go of Galgo. As Tishimi landed on her feet her two swords disemboweled and beheaded the harpy. She helped Galgo to his feet. He bled from both shoulders, but was not badly hurt.

"*Arigato,*" he said to Tishimi, collapsing to his knees.

Sinbad scanned the sky, one hand shading his eyes. But there were no more harpies.

Suddenly the Blue Nymph listed to port as one of the *peris* vanished.

Men screamed, fell and rolled against the deck. All but poor, wounded Ajib managed to grab onto something for support. Before any of the crew could reach him in time to help him, he tumbled over the ship's rail and plummeted to a dark and watery grave. One of the remaining two *peris* on that side grabbed the fallen chain and righted the ship. The others paid no attention to what had occurred.

When it was done and over, Sinbad and what remained of his crew, including Bharat and Urmila, gathered around Galgo and Tishimi.

"Look!" said Henri, pointing to the head the magicman had brought on deck.

Everyone turned to where the head lay. No longer a woman's head with writhing serpents and yellow eyes, it was nothing more than the head of the canisaur Galgo had placed in the bag the night the creatures had invaded his house.

"My compliments to you, Galgo," Bharat remarked.

"How is it that we were not also turned to stone?" asked Ralf.

"The spell I cast to create the illusion also protected each one of you," Galgo told him.

"The harpies believed the illusion was real," Rafi explained. "Their fear of Medusa's gaze lent power to the illusion."

"Very astute observation," Urmila told him.

"I guess that canisaur head proved its worth after all," said Sinbad, bowing to the magicman. He wondered how and why the scholar and his daughter had escaped harm and death. He decided to say nothing for the time being, however. There were other matters at hand.

The Blue Nymph suddenly listed to starboard, and the crew and their guests were thrown to the deck again and began sliding toward that side of the vessel. Another *peri* had vanished. Not a moment later one of the *peris* off the starboard bow grabbed the abandoned chain and the ship righted itself again. Once everyone had regained their feet, Sinbad helped Galgo to stand.

"What is going wrong?" he asked the magicman. "Why are the *peris* vanishing?"

"I have lost too much blood," Galgo explained. "The Medusa illusion weakened me, and thus I begin to lose power and control over the *peris*. I pray we reach the island safely."

"Take him below and see to his wounds, Rafi," said Sinbad. "Then you can tend to the rest of us." He turned his eyes toward Heaven and prayed to Allah to have mercy on them and guide them to a safe landing at the island.

"Captain!" Haroun shouted from the crow's next. "I see it! I see the island!" He pointed off to starboard, pointed down toward the sea.

Everyone gathered at the rail and stared. Far, far below, Sinbad spotted a small island, completely surrounded by white mist.

"We have made excellent time," said Bharat. "We shall land before nightfall. Then we can rest and start off first thing in the morning."

"Praise and all thanks to Allah, the Just and Merciful!" shouted Sinbad.

And then, as gentle as could be, the five remaining *peris* began to descend, and the Blue Nymph drew closer and closer to the island.

Come morning, Sinbad and his shore party prepared to go ashore.

The Blue Nymph lay at anchor, just off shore of the nameless isle. Behind and all around her lay the treacherous barrier reef, and beyond that, surrounding the island, hung the strange, white mist. The five remaining *peris* were as still as sentinels, standing in the shallows, guarding their posts. The turquoise water was almost translucent, and the morning sun stood like a great white eye burning a hole in the blue vault of Heaven.

As the shore party readied to depart, Amahd appeared on deck, his eyes as bright a yellow as the sun. But now his flesh had become jaundiced, too.

"I told you before," Sinbad said to him. "You are *not* coming with us."

Amahd leaned against the ship's rail, where Omar, Haroun, Rafi, Badar, and what remained of the small crew had gathered.

"But I am the caliph's cousin!" he protested.

"*Third* cousin," said Henri.

"Twice removed," Ralf added.

"But Galgo is going with you and he's wounded!" Amahd argued.

"I'm not badly hurt, whereas you are still quite ill," said the magicman.

The look the humpbacked dwarf cast at Galgo was villainous and vengeful, thought Sinbad. But he put it down as a result of Amahd's illness.

"He is needed, you are not," Tishimi told Amahd, turning her back and wading ashore.

Amahd refused to give it up. "But Captain…"

"I grow weary of your whining and pleading and disobedience," said

Sinbad. He turned to Badar. "Keep an eye on him. Lock him in the hold, if you have to."

"That I will," said Badar.

"Omar, I leave you in charge," said Sinbad. "Rafi, you're in charge of Omar."

"What about me?" Haroun asked.

"Keep to your nest, little bird!" Omar told him.

So Sinbad and Tishimi, along with Henri, Ralf, Bharat, Urmila and Galgo, went ashore to find the Golden Fleece.

The island was as silent as night on a calm sea. There were no trees, no grass or vegetation of any kind. It was all sand and barren rock, like a great stone that had been set in the middle of the sea. No birds or other life did they see or hear, and the white mist surrounded the island like a wall of clouds. The beach gave way to a headland, and soon they were making their way across a barren plain of rock and gravel that sloped gently upward, the ground as dry as an old bone. Sinbad felt that they landed in a realm set apart from the rest of the outside world.

Their trek continued for some hours, until they finally reached a cliff overlooking the sea at the other end of the island. There they came upon a massive stone arch with five steps leading to a pair of great wooden doors. The curious structure had no walls or roof, and it stood at the very edge of the cliff.

"This makes no sense at all," said Galgo. "Where's the rest of the building?"

Sinbad thought this far stranger than the pyramid in the land of Hyperborea. "Perhaps part of the island tumbled into the sea and took the temple with it, leaving only the entrance?"

"Only one way to find out," said Ralf. He walked up the steps and pushed on the doors. They opened with little resistance, save for the sound of rusted hinges. "By Odin's One Eye!"

The others raced up the stairs to join him.

"And Allah's Beard!" said Sinbad.

Beyond the doors, *inside*, as it were, they beheld a vast stretch of grassland, and beyond that, a lush, tropical rainforest. Though they saw no signs of life, they did hear the song of birds, the chatter of monkeys, and the calls of other animals coming from deep within the forest. Not far off in the distance, they could see a stone structure built to resemble a large grotto.

"More of Medea's magic?" asked Rafi.

"Hecate, Helios and Circe taught her well," Urmila replied.

"*Too* well, I'm afraid," Bharat told him. "For even those three could not find this place."

"With her dying breath, Medea enspelled the island and all the artifacts and relics she had stolen, and hid everything from the eyes of the gods of Mount Olympus," Urmila explained.

"There is no god but Allah," said Sinbad.

"There is more to Allah's creation than you can imagine," Urmila told him. "All things are fashioned by his hand, even those who were once worshipped as gods in other lands."

"Even my gods?" Ralf asked her.

"Even your gods, Norseman."

Sinbad was about to say something else when Tishimi spoke up.

"What the woman says may be true, Sinbad," said she. "If there is only one God, then he is the source of all life. Who can say what other worlds, what other forms of life he created, but in his wisdom has chosen to keep hidden from the eyes of men?"

Bharat coughed into his hand. "I hate to interrupt this discussion, but if we are to find what we came here in search of, I don't think standing around talking will do us any good."

"Then let us proceed," said Sinbad.

With no further conversation, he led his crew and passengers through the gates. When he glanced over his shoulder, he expected to see the doors close behind them. To his relief, the arch and the open doors were still there. They had, indeed, entered another world.

In silence they trekked across that serene landscape and the short distance to the grotto. Inside the stone structure, they found a stone altar heaped with ancient relics, scrolls, tablets, plates, and vases. Two palm-like trees bearing golden apples stood on either side of the grotto like a pair of arboreal sentinels. Piled on each side of the altar were more artifacts: weapons and armor and such to the left; on the right, hundreds of small, plain-looking wooden boxes, each one identical to the others, and all neatly stacked.

"These are the treasures that Medea stole," Urmila explained. "Here you will find the spear and armor of Achilles, and the weapons of Heracles."

There were other artifacts, as well, and Urmila, scholar that she was, named some of them: the Helm of Darkness, the Aegis shield of Perseus, and the sword Harpe, which he had used to slay Medusa. Here, too, were the bow of Artemis, the shield of Ajax, the arrow that struck down Achilles, and the girdle of Hippolyta, Queen of the Amazons. Many other treasures there were, the wealth of ancient Greece, the treasure of the gods of Mount Olympus.

"I regret leaving Rafi behind," Sinbad lamented. "He would have relished all this."

Bharat pointed to the great stack of wooden boxes. "I believe Pandora's Box may be found among those."

"But they are all alike!" said Henri. "How can we find the correct one?"

"And where is the Golden Fleece?" asked Sinbad. "I see nothing that looks like the head and hide of a golden ram."

"One thing at a time, Captain," Galgo told him.

The magicman walked over to the boxes and stood there for a moment, staring at them and rubbing his chin. He reached a hand inside a pocket of his robe, and slowly removed his clenched fist. Uttering a strange word, he waved his arm and unclenched his fist. Wincing from the pain of his wounded shoulders, he threw a cloud of brown dust over the stack of boxes. Not a moment later the boxes shimmered and began to vanish from sight until all but one remained.

Galgo picked up the box, rejoined the others and handed it to Urmila. "Chiastolite dust," he explained. "It is used to dispel illusions."

"Excellent and well done," Urmila told him.

Bharat took the box from his daughter. He opened it and showed it to the others.

"It's empty!" said Ralf.

"Of course it is," Urmila told him. "When Pandora first opened the box, she unleashed all the ills and evils it had contained."

"Then the Fleece must be here, as well," said Henri.

"Even in light of all that we have seen and encountered, I am still not convinced that such a thing as the skin of a golden ram exists," said Sinbad.

"Perhaps it was also hidden or disguised with magic," said Tishimi.

"Perhaps," said Urmila.

Henri then removed a leather bag from inside his shirt and walked toward one of the trees bearing the golden apples.

"What do you think you're doing?" Sinbad asked him.

The archer grinned. "We came here in search of the Golden Fleece so why should we not return with a few golden apples as well, no?"

At that moment Sinbad and his company heard the distant roar of some great beast, a roar that echoed from deep inside the grotto. It reminded him somewhat of the roar of the one-eyed centaur he had fought and slain on the lost continent of Lemuria.

"Henri, get back here and ready your bow!" shouted Tishimi, drawing her *katana.*

Sinbad unsheathed his sword. "Bharat, Urmila, Galgo, stay well behind us!"

As those three retreated, Ralf drew his broadsword. "Henri, if you don't get back here I'll strangle you with your own bowstring!"

Henri quickly plucked three apples and stuffed them inside the leather bag just as another roar sounded and an ancient creature emerged from deep within the shadows of the grotto.

"An *ophiotaurus!*" Urmila cried.

A monster straight out of ancient Greek myth, the ophiotaurus possessed the head and forelegs of a bull, and the body of a serpent. Massive, it was, too, as long as two stallions and as tall as a Cretan bull. Its two bronze horns gleamed in the sunlight and were twice the length of a man's arm. It snorted, shook its great head, pawed the ground and then...

"Henri...move!" yelled Sinbad.

The beast charged, straight at the archer from Gaul.

Henri moved a split moment before the horns of the beast skewered him. But he did not move fast enough. One horn grazed his left buttock, opening a shallow wound. Then the whip-like tail of the thing lashed out and battered him aside. He flew across the chamber, crashed into a large bush and dropped to the ground. He did not get up again.

"Odin!" Ralf yelled as he raced forward.

The ophiotaurus did not falter in its advance. It wheeled about and charged straight for Ralf. The monster shook its head and swatted the air with its tail. The big Viking turned aside at the last moment and struck the creature across the back of the neck with his broadsword. The ophiotaurus bellowed in pain. Bright green blood splashed the air. Yet even that powerful stroke and great blade could not cleave through the beast's thickly-muscled neck. Ralf dropped to the ground and rolled out of the way as the monster made to ram him with its head and gore him with its horns. Ralf was on his feet within moments, plunging his sword into the creature's side. But he forgot about the thing's tail, which whipped around and coiled itself around his body.

"Ralf!" Sinbad shouted.

Wrapped tightly in the coils of the monster's tail, Ralf struggled to break free. His arms were trapped against his sides, however, and though he still gripped his sword, it was of little use to him. The beast whipped him back and forth in the air as if he were a child's plaything. Sinbad sprang

The beast charged the archer from Gaul.

forward to assault the left side of the ophiotaurus. Tishimi unsheathed her *tanto*, and with both big and small swords now in hand, she struck at the monster's right flank. In a blind rage born of pain, the ophiotaurus did not know which assailant to attack.

Taking advantage of the thing's confusion, Sinbad drove his sword into the side of the creature. Out of the corner of his eye he caught sight of Ralf high in the air, in the grip of the monster's tail as it swung him back and forth. Sinbad ducked barely in time to avoid being swatted like a fly by that serpent tail and the Viking's brawny body. But the ophiotaurus chose that moment to turn its attack upon Tishimi, and the sudden alteration in its course yanked the sword from Sinbad's hand. Not missing a beat, he threw himself on top of the creature. He landed in a sitting position behind the great bull head. Wishing that his magical dagger, Grachene, would choose that moment to appear in his sash, he did the only thing he could: he took the bull by the horns and sweated and strained as he pulled back on its massive head.

Meanwhile, Tishimi danced back and forth, avoiding the charge of the bull, striking it first with her *katana*, then moving aside and striking next with her shorter sword. Deep wounds to the beast's head and shoulder were inflicted by those two deadly blades. The ophiotaurus bellowed and hissed as blood spewed. While Sinbad attacked the beast with his sword, Tishimi leapt into the air, stabbing the massive bull's head with her short blade, slicing its neck with her *katana*. But the beast would not go down. Agile as a cat, she landed on her feet and spun around just as Sinbad landed on the back of the ophiotaurus, took hold of its two horns, and began to pull back on its head, exposing its throat.

"Any time now, Tishimi!" he said.

Tishimi rushed in for the kill. Her two swords flashed. The *tanto* slashed open the neck of the ophiotaurus, her father's sword she plunged into its heart. With a great roar, the monster shook and trembled. Its forelegs buckled and it collapsed. The great tail loosened its grip and Ralf dropped to the ground. Sinbad leapt free and retrieved his sword. Drawing his axe, Ralf swung the great weapon and, with one mighty blow, cleaved the bull's head in half. Heaving a great, painful sigh, the ophiotaurus rolled over onto its side, dead. The serpent's tail shook in the air like a drunken cobra for a few moments, and then fell limp to the ground.

Sinbad and Tishimi exchanged bows. Henri limped toward them.

"Did that dim your passion for gold?" Ralf asked him.

Henri scowled at the big Viking. "Did that not teach you the meaning of fear?"

"Is everyone all right?" asked Sinbad.

"My ribs hurt," said Ralf.

Henri bent over to show them his ripped trousers and wounded buttock. "I do not think I will be sitting down for some time."

Tishimi rolled her eyes. "Men," she mumbled with disgust, sheathing her two swords.

Bharat, Urmila and Galgo walked over to them.

"This is a sad day, Sinbad. You have slain the last of a rare and forgotten breed of ancient creatures," said Urmila.

"It's not like we had much choice, by Allah's Beard!" he said.

The body of the ophiotaurus underwent a sudden and curious transformation. The bull's head and the serpent's body began to glow with a shimmering, amber light. Then it began to shrink in size, to change shape and form.

Within moments it revealed itself to be the head and fleece of a golden ram.

No one said a word for several moments. In that space, Sinbad walked forward, hesitantly, wondering if the Golden Fleece was safe to touch, to pick up.

"So this is how Medea hid the Fleece from our eyes," said Bharat, exchanging smiles and knowing looks with his daughter.

"Medea's magic must have been powerful indeed," Sinbad remarked.

"You have no idea," Urmila said to him.

"More illusions! Is nothing on this island what it appears to be?" Henri wondered aloud.

"This was not an illusion," said Bharat, his eyes darting from Urmila to Henri. "This was a shape-shifting spell, undone only with the death of the ophiotaurus."

Tishimi had been quick to note Bharat's words and the exchange between him and his daughter. She held her silence, but continued watching them closely.

"Pick up the Fleece, Sinbad," Urmila said. "Bring it here."

Sinbad sheathed his sword and then knelt beside the Golden Fleece. His hands shook as he reached for it. He did not know what to expect when he touched it, but the warmth that radiated from it proved pleasant and comforting.

Then he heard a familiar howling, and rose quickly to his feet. He spun around just as a raging canisaur charged through the open doors of the arch and headed straight for Galgo.

Tishimi saw it and shouted warning. "Galgo, look out!"

She made to draw her swords, but fast as she was, she was not quick enough. Before her hands touched hilts the canisaur plowed into her, its talons slashing her shoulder with a grievous wound. Blood spurted and she fell to her knees. Then, before anyone else had time to react, the canisaur had seized Galgo, sinking its teeth into his throat, ripping it to shreds. He did not have time to scream before the monster ripped off his head.

Sinbad tossed the Fleece to Ralf, drew his sword and charged in. Just as his blade cut into the canisaur's neck, an arrow *whooshed* past him and buried itself in the thing's skull. The vicious beast fell over dead, soaked in the blood of the magicman, and in its own blood, as well. Although he was long dead, Galgo's sorcerous rival had taken his revenge.

Heart pounding, Sinbad hurried to Tishimi's side. Blood poured from her wound. The others gathered around. Henri and Ralf knelt beside her, each taking one of her hands.

"You'll be fine," Sinbad told her. "The wound is deep, but it will not claim your life."

Though her face was pale and her eyes dark, Tishimi managed a weak smile.

"Whether she lives or dies is not an issue," said Urmila. "She has been infected by the poisonous claws of the canisaur, and in a matter of a few days she will turn."

"What do you mean, she will *turn*?" Ralf demanded.

Sinbad guessed, he knew, and his heart sank. "She will become one of those things."

No further words were spoken, for just then Rafi raced through the opened doors of the arch, running across the field of grass toward where they were gathered. His face was flushed and his eyes wide with amazement as he took in his surroundings. Then he slid to a stop when he saw how sorely Tishimi had been wounded.

"Captain! How…what happened?" he cried.

"Tishimi was badly hurt trying to save Galgo from that monster's attack," Sinbad told him, nodding over his shoulder to where lay the bodies of the magicman and the canisaur.

Rafi glanced to where his captain pointed, and then his eyes went wide. "There is no monster there, Sinbad, only the bodies of Amahd and the magician."

Sinbad and the others turned around. "May Allah save us!" he cried.
"More foul magic!" Ralf growled.

"Amahd, he was wounded, that night in Galgo's house," said Tishimi.
She bit her bottom lip in pain, but would not allow a cry to escape her lips.

It was obvious to Sinbad that Galgo had not known that the wound
Amahd had received from the canisaur had been the cause of the dwarf
prince's illness. "Rafi, what happened?" he asked. "Amahd was told to
stay aboard the Nymph."

"I went to see how he was feeling, only to find him gone and poor Badar
slain, his throat torn out," Rafi explained. "Then I saw a strange creature,
like a hound, leap from the railing of the ship and head this way. The others
saw it, too."

"Do what you can to stop Tishimi's wound from bleeding," Sinbad told
him. "Then we must get her back to the ship."

"Nothing you can do will save her, Captain," said Urmila.

"*Mon Dieu,* that cannot be," said Henri. "I had thought that for as long
as she owns her father's sword, no magic can oppose her blade or harm
her."

"The canisaur is a demon, not a creature born of magic, and no magic
is involved in what will happen to her in a few days," said Urmila. "She
is infected."

Sinbad leapt to his feet and turned angrily upon the woman. "If you
know so much about these matters, then what do we do? How do we save
her?"

Urmila glanced at her father, and then held out her hands to Sinbad.
"Give me the Golden Fleece, Captain. That is her only hope."

Concerned for Tishimi's life, Sinbad did not hesitate in handing the
Fleece to Urmila.

"Be still now, Tishimi," said Urmila, wrapping her in the Golden Fleece.

Tishimi's eyes closed, and then the golden sheen of the Fleece faded,
became dull as if it were tarnished. Her pale face became flushed, but
not more than a few moments later her color returned to normal and she
opened her eyes. When Urmila removed the Fleece from Tishimi, the only
evidence that she had been wounded at all were the bloodstains on her torn
black silk blouse. Rafi helped her to stand, and she bowed to Urmila, who
bowed in return. The Fleece, Sinbad noticed, began to shine again like
polished gold.

"Praise Allah!" he said. "But how do we know that the infection will
not claim her?"

"You must have faith, Sinbad," Urmila said. "You must *believe*."

Tishimi eyed Urmila and Bharat. "I think it time you reveal who you truly are."

"You know?" asked Bharat.

"She has been suspicious of us ever since we set out on this journey," said Urmila.

Father and daughter nodded to each other, and then their bodies began to melt, their flesh pouring from them like wax melting from a burning candle.

Sinbad and his crew stepped back several paces, not knowing what would next happen. Only Tishimi remained where she stood.

Where the old, bearded Bharat had been there now stood a tall, thin man, clean-shaven and of early middle years, dressed in a simple white tunic and sandals. A beautiful young woman with golden hair, fair skin and blue eyes had replaced Urmila. She wore a flowing white robe, embroidered with gold. The Fleece she still held in her hands.

"Hermes and Hera, I presume?" asked Rafi.

"We have been known by those names," said the woman who had called herself Urmila.

Sinbad could not believe what his eyes had just seen. Now he understood why the harpies had not attacked them aboard the Blue Nymph. "You...you are the gods of ancient Greece?"

"In ancient times we were worshipped as such," Hermes who had been Bharat told him. "And many of our own people came to believe themselves to be gods."

"We are no more gods than you are, Sinbad," said Hera. "We are merely blessed with longer lives than you, but we are not immortal,"

"Then from where do you come?" he asked.

Hera smiled mischievously, and her eyes twinkled. "Let us just say that we come from the land beyond Beyond."

Sinbad felt like a man who had fallen overboard. "But why did you not reveal yourselves to us sooner?"

"We were forbidden to do so," Bharat replied.

For over a thousand years, Hera explained, she and Hermes had wandered the world, searching for the Golden Fleece. They had helped Jason in his original quest, and thus set into motion the chain of events that had caused a vengeful Medea to hide it away. But then one night, thirty years earlier, Pallas Athena, daughter of Zeus, had a strange dream.

"Athena had a vision of this island and drew the map that guided us here," said Hera. "She said that a man named Sinbad El Ari, who would lose a sandal in his quest to find the Golden Fleece, just as Jason of old once lost a sandal, would help us find the Fleece." Again she smiled at Sinbad, knowingly, this time. "Did you not recently lose one of your sandals?"

"Why, yes…yes, I did," he said, remembering back to when he had found the blue rose. "But why did you need my help, when all along Athena knew how to find this island?"

"Because the night Athena had her dream was the same night you were born, Sinbad," said Hermes. "Because in her dream the voice of a Muse told her that we could not reclaim the Golden Fleece until the hand of Sinbad El Ari touched it first."

"So it was the Fleece you really wanted," Sinbad said, angrily, "and not Pandora's Box?"

"Peace, Sinbad," Tishimi said. "The Fleece has always been rightfully theirs, and with it, Hera was able to save my life."

Hera smiled gratefully at the swordswoman. "The Fleece is more than a valued treasure to my people," she said. "It is a source of power. We have great need of it, for without it we will never be able to return to our own place in the Universe. We wish to go home, Sinbad. That is all we want. I'm certain you can understand that. It is our one and only hope."

In spite of himself, Sinbad felt his anger abate. Gods or not, he had no wish to fight them over the Fleece. Too much blood had already been spilled, and too many good men had already died. And as wise Tishimi had pointed out, her life had been saved by Hera.

"Then we return to Baghdad with no treasure for the Caliph," he said. "And the hand of Princess Yasmina will be given to the Sultan of Oman."

"You will not return empty handed," said Hermes, handing Pandora's Box to Sinbad.

"But there is nothing in this box!" said Sinbad.

Hera touched the box and then opened it. Inside it was the withered blue rose.

"How…how did you get this?" he asked.

With a smile of mystery gracing her lovely face, Hera touched the blue rose and it came back to life, healthy and strong and vibrant of color.

"Hammer of Thor!" said Ralf.

"Bring this to your Caliph," said Hera. "Tell him that Hope is worth far more than the value of anything made of gold. Never lose that which resides in your heart, Sinbad."

Sinbad understood. He could no more lose Hope than he could lose his desire for beautiful women, his love for the Blue Nymph, and his lust for adventurer.

"We must now depart," said Hermes. "Farewell, my friends and thank you!"

"As for you, Henri, you may keep those three golden apples but only those three, as a token of our gratitude," said Hera.

"*Merci, mademoiselle,*" Henri said graciously.

"What will now happen to this island and all its treasures?" asked Rafi.

"In time it will fade from your memories and cease to exist," Bharat replied.

Hera bowed to Sinbad. "Goodbye, Son of Ari. You are greatly favored by Allah."

The Golden Fleece began to shine even more brightly now, even brighter than the sun. Sinbad and his crew were forced to close their eyes against the intensity of the Fleece's golden sheen. Even so, they could still see something of that brilliant radiance. But then the light began to fade, and once it had faded, they opened their eyes again.

Hera and Hermes were no longer among them.

Henri crossed himself and then kissed his fingers.

"Come, let us bury Galgo and poor Amahd, and then return to the Nymph," said Sinbad. "I have had enough of this place and pagan gods or djinn or whatever they were."

"But there's loot to be had!" said Ralf.

"We cannot leave such treasures here, Capitaine!" Henri agreed. "You heard; soon this island will no longer be here!"

Sinbad had a feeling that it would be best for them to heed Hera's words and not tempt Fate. "No, Allah does not favor greedy men."

It was not a long trek back to the beach where the Blue Nymph lay anchored, just off shore, but even before they reached her, they could see that something was wrong.

"The *peris*...they're gone!" Sinbad cried out in dismay.

Indeed it was so. The descendants of the fallen angels who had carried the Blue Nymph through the clouds and to the island of the Golden Fleece were no longer there. Only the great chains remained, hanging from the ship and lying in the shallows.

Sinbad and company raced down to the beach, where Omar, Haroun, and what remained of the crew were sitting, staring at the ship and the white mist that surrounded the island.

"Omar, what happened to the *peris*?" he asked.

The First Mate shrugged. "I have no idea," he said. "One moment they were here, as still and silent as the mountains and the next, they vanished!"

"It happened not long after you went off chasing that creature, Rafi," said Haroun.

Sinbad then remembered what had happened aboard the Blue Nymph, after the battle with the harpies, when Galgo had been wounded. "With Galgo's death, the spell was cancelled and the *peris* were freed from his service."

Haroun looked around. "Where's Amahd? And the others?"

"I'll tell you the tale later, lad, over a tankard of ale," Ralf told him.

"So now we have a very long voyage ahead of us, with a very small crew," said Omar.

"May Allah grant we find our way home," said Rafi.

"And may Allah grant we find nothing else," Sinbad added.

"But how do we navigate through the mist and past the barrier reef?" asked Omar.

Just as he and the others began to despair, the clouds parted and a shaft of golden sunlight poured down from Heaven. A moment later, a score of white, winged stallions, each wearing some sort of harness, descended from the sky.

"The *pegasi!*" cried Rafi. "The Children of Pegasus!"

"Gifts from Hera and Hermes, no doubt," said Tishimi.

"Looks like the Blue Nymph will become a flying ship once more!" said Sinbad.

"Wonderful," Henri said without enthusiasm, shaking his head. "I wonder how badly the Caliph will take the news that his cousin Amahd is no longer among the living."

"I think the loss of the Golden Fleece will sadden him much more," said Ralf.

Tishimi shook her head and mumbled something about men.

Rafi laid a hand on Sinbad's shoulder. "Do you think the Caliph will accept Pandora's Box in place of the Golden Fleece and give the hand of Princess Yasmina to you in marriage?"

Sinbad opened the lid of Pandora's Box and stared at the blue rose tucked neatly inside it.

"One can always hope so, Rafi. One can always hope."

THE END

Sinbad and Me

I was six years-old in 1958. Life was a waking dream filled with magic, mystery, and wonder. It was a year that would have a profound impact on my young life, one that would still be affecting me 50-some years later. I had already seen the original *King Kong* and *Mighty Joe Young* on television, thanks to my Dad and his love for the pulps and stop-motion animation. There was also another, very important film I saw that year, one that not only blew me out of my seat, but inspired a whole new generation of Special FX artists.

I'm talking about Ray Harryhausen's masterpiece, *The 7ᵗʰ Voyage of Sinbad,* of course.

To see this film on the big widescreen, viewing it through six year-old eyes, is one of my most cherished cinematic memories. From the moment that big cyclops appears on screen I was transported to a whole new world. Bernard Herrmann's wonderful score set the perfect tone and heightened the magic of this all-time classic. From a handmaid turned into a snake-woman, a shrunken princess, a pair of cyclopes, and a fire-spitting dragon, to a giant Roc and her babies, a genie, magic potions, an evil sorcerer, and that most incredible and famous sword-fighting scene between Sinbad and the skeleton—I was transfixed. I own and love all Harryhausen's films, but the three Sinbad films stand apart from the others. Only one other film, his second masterpiece, *Jason and the Argonauts* inspired and moved me so deeply. Ray Harryhausen is present, and "contributes" at least one cameo moment, in almost everything I've written and published to date, and that includes my space opera, *Three Against The Stars,* also published by Airship 27 Productions. There is no way for me to really write any kind of fantasy or "mythic adventure" story *without* designing some creature that I can imagine RH animating for one of his films.

So . . . when Ron Fortier asked me if I would be interested in contributing a story to the first volume of *Sinbad: The New Voyages*, I was thrilled—and I was also a bit perplexed. I could not come up with anything, plus I was in the middle of finishing one novel and starting work on a novella for another anthology. Thus, I took a rain check, deciding to wait for the first book in the series to come out so I could see what the other writers had done, see how they handled the characters, the dialogue and "voices," and how they told their stories.

Flashback to 1998: I wrote a screenplay called *Sinbad's Summer Vacation.* It was a tribute to Ray Harryhausen, both a parody and homage to his Sinbad films, and a mash-up of those with *Jason and The Argonauts.* I had even planned to send him the script as a gift, for at I have two good friends who knew him quite well, and remained close friends with him until his recent passing. Oddly enough, my script contained a Viking (from Minnesota), and a samurai warrior—both named after fictional characters created by two friends of mine. There were other characters in the story, too: a Native American, two modern-day female characters inspired by the television shows *Bewitched* and *I Dream of Jeannie,* and even The Three Stooges in the form of The Moronis Brothers—Colitis (Moe), Gastritis (Larry) and Gesundheit (Curly.) I even "borrowed" some ideas from Popeye the Sailor's own version of Sinbad, as well as his take on Aladdin and Ali Baba. My plot was straightforward: Sinbad, as well as all these characters from different centuries and eras, falls into a hole in the Space-Time continuum and ends up in ancient Greece, shortly after the death of Jason and the disappearance of the Golden Fleece. Now, in order for him and the others to return to their own lands and their own times, they must find the Golden Fleece. In order for them to find the Fleece, they have to help a mysterious sorcerer find Pandora's Box. That's it. It was old-school slapstick comedy adventure featuring a lot of special FX and my favorite creation—the *Kankersaurus.* Sadly, I never finished the final draft of the second version of the script.

Flash forward to 2013: I read the first volume of *Sinbad: The New Voyages,* and fell in love with the characters and stories. Then the light bulb goes off in my head. What if I took the germ of the plot from my old Sinbad script—the Golden Fleece and Pandora's Box—and wrote a whole new tale around it? I mentioned it to Ron, he sent me the Sinbad story "bible," and off I went sailing aboard the Blue Nymph with the Sindhi captain and his crew, and with a few of my own characters written exclusively for this story. And that's how *Sinbad and the Golden Fleece* came to life. It was a fun story to write, and challenging in some aspects because I was writing about characters that were not created by me. Plus, three excellent stories had already been published. But what Nancy Hansen, Derrick Ferguson and I.A. Watson set down in the first volume guided my course, and Ron's great characters were most agreeable and cooperative. Without any of them, I would not have been able to do it.

Without Ray Harryhausen, none of us would be writing of Sinbad's new voyages.

I hope I get a chance to visit these characters again.

JOE BONADONNA -has thus far published three books: the heroic fantasy collection, *Mad Shadows: The Weird Tales of Dorgo the Dowser*, published by iUniverse; the space opera, *Three Against The Stars*, published by Airship27 Productions; and *Waters of Darkness*, a sword and sorcery pirate adventure, in collaboration with David C. Smith, and published by Damnation Books. He has stories appearing in Heathen Oracle's *Azieran: Artifacts and Relics; GRIOTS 2: Sisters of the Spear*, from by MVmedia; and Janet Morris' *Poets in Hell*, from Perseid Press. Joe has written a number of articles and book reviews for Black Gate Magazine, and is an administrator for the Facebook groups *The Swords and Sorcery League, The Swords and Planet League,* and *Bonadonna's Bookshelf.* You can find Joe on Facebook and Google+. His blog, which he often fails to update, can be found at www.dorgoland.blogspot.com. Visit his Amazon Author's page, too!

Sinbad and the Scorpion God

By Ralph L. Angelo Jr.

Sinbad El Ari stood at the bow of his ship, 'The Blue Nymph'. His right foot up on the rail, a huge grin plastered across his dark, handsome features. Sinbad was a sailor born. The smell of salt was not just in his nostrils, it was in his veins. He did not just enjoy being at sea, he relished it.

The Blue Nymph cleaved the ocean, a shower of saltwater sprayed against Sinbad's van dyke bearded face and chest. His black skin glistened with it, and he smiled. But not all was right for Sinbad even though he was content at the moment. Sinbad's mind drifted back to earlier, back at the port of Kahoun, a small seaside town known for shady dealing. Sinbad, his first mate Omar, the burly Norseman Ralf Gunarson and the wiry Gaul archer Henri Delacrois sat around a table in a small pub.

"You drink much this day, Henri Delacrois," Ralf observed, "Does something bother you?"

"You are observant mon ami. Today is the anniversary of the day I left my village behind. It was five long years ago today that I decided to make my way into the greater world."

Sinbad smirked in that boyish way of his, with a sparkle to his dark blue eyes, "Do you not mean Henri, today is the anniversary of the day you were run out of the village by the mayor's guards after being found in bed with his wife? If you did not run a hangman's noose would have been your next stop within that village."

"Ah Sinbad, thank you, yet once again for reminding me of my, shall we say, mes erreurs? You are a true boon campagnon."

Three of the men laughed, only Omar scowled, while taking another pull of his tankard. "Allah will take no pleasure in hearing you fools."

Sinbad turned toward him and smiled, "Nor does he suffer those who indulge in forbidden beverages, such as we all are right now." Sinbad raised his own tankard and clanked it hard against Ralf's.

"I can beg forgiveness at the hour of my death. Allah can be reasonable, or so it is said."

"Enough of this talk of gods; I wish to see women dance." Gunarson commented. He turned his bulk in his much too small seat toward the stage in the center of the bar, where a lithe dancer, her face covered in veils took the stage and began to gyrate seductively.

"Ah Sinbad, what I would give for a night of pleasure with such a woman, eh?" Henri spoke in a low voice.

"Shh, Henri. Enjoy the show. There are plenty of women here for you to get in trouble with." Sinbad muttered, his eyes not leaving the stage and a grin plastered on his face.

The four men continued to watch the comely maiden sinuously writhe on the small stage. But something caught Ralf Gunarson's battle hardened senses ere long. The big Viking had a feeling. A vague sense all was not right within the tavern.

Ralf turned his head slightly and out of the corner of his eye saw armed guards of the city entering the pub at every entrance and exit, blocking all escape.

"Sinbad," he hissed, shaking his captain's arm.

"Hhmm? What is it? Ralf?" Sinbad answered distractedly.

"Look to the doors, man. Look!"

Sinbad turned his head not so much to be noticeable, but just enough that he saw what his trusted companion was speaking of.

"Omar, Henri, gird yourselves. The palace guard is here, and they are staring at the four of us."

Omar looked annoyingly at Sinbad, "Why does Allah curse me yet again? What have you done this time, Sinbad?"

The guardsmen began to move on their table, but Sinbad and his cohorts immediately stood. Each pulled a blade from its scabbard with Ralf Gunarson lifting a double bladed axe he had placed beneath the table, to hold it before himself.

The four men stood with their backs to the table itself facing the now uncertain guardsmen, "What do you wish of us, guards?" Sinbad began, "We have done no wrong, at least not in this port." A nervous laugh circulated through the crowd.

The head of the guardsmen stepped forth, "You are Sinbad of the Blue Nymph? Currently moored at our town dock?"

Sinbad bowed his turbaned head, "At your service, sir. Again I ask what do you wish of us?"

"The Caliph of Kahoun wishes an audience with you, and lest you make the error of thinking otherwise, this is not a request."

"And if we refuse? You out number us four to one, Captain of the guard. I hardly think the odds are fair for a fight."

"Then do not fight us and you will not be harmed." the Captain replied.

"I was not speaking of the odds being in your favor, Captain, but rather in ours."

The four men of the Blue Nymph exploded away from the table simultaneously, driving forth into the startled guardsmen. Each man drove forward toward an exit, slashing and hacking their way toward freedom. Sinbad smiled all the while, his curved scimitar rose and fell repeatedly, forcing the stunned guardsmen back with lightning quick slashes; keeping them on their heels, but doing no permanent damage. Leaping atop a table, Sinbad spun and parried a slashing blade, stepped sideways and kicked the blades owner in the jaw as he leaped past him and grabbed onto a swinging chandelier of candles. He kicked his legs out far, swung above the heads of his enemies, and released the chandelier which pulled free of the ceiling of the place, dropping wood and debris from the ceiling upon the guardsmen's heads.

With a jaunty laugh, Sinbad landed near an exit, behind more of the guardsmen whose heads he had just sailed over.

Next arrived Henri Delacrois at Sinbad's side, together the two men began to battle the horde of guardsmen who had just turned and realized the men they had been sent to take into custody were now standing between them and the exit.

"Fancy meeting you here, eh mon ami?" Delacrois grunted between sword strokes

"Where are the others?" Sinbad asked stoically.

"When last I saw the giant Norseman he had half a dozen of our playmates held at bay. Omar was at his back."

As if in response to Sinbad's query a beastly howl exploded from across the bar, followed by men cursing and shouting. Sinbad stole a glance from his own harried sword battle and saw bodies begin to sail overhead, clearing a path toward another exit.

"Out the door, Henri, quickly. Our Norse bull is making a break for it."

Delacrois nodded and slipped out into the dark alleyway, followed quickly by a rolling Sinbad. Quickly the sailor sprang to his feet and with Delacrois' help, pushed a large wooden trash bin in front of the doorway.

Both men turned and ran, followed by screams of anger as the guards opened the door and fell directly into the garbage bin that had been placed in their path.

Sinbad and Henri smirked as they ran.

"Quickly, this way." Sinbad commanded, "Ralf should be exiting there at any moment."

The door exploded outward, shattered by the massive double headed axe of Ralf Gunarson.

Almost instantly Ralf and Omar followed it through the door, Ralf stooping low to retrieve the thrown blade.

"To the Nymph!" Sinbad ordered.

The four men ran through back alleys, taking a circuitous route back to their ship.

"The ship is strangely silent. I see no guards on duty, by Allah. I like this not." Omar muttered.

"Just be on your guard, all of you." Sinbad hissed.

The four men stealthily stole along the deck, heading toward the below deck cabins. Sinbad entered first. Silent as a mouse he padded down a dark corridor toward the crew cabins when a door he had just passed creaked open. He spun quickly, but not quickly enough. The back of his head exploded in pain. Sinbad fell to his knees and rolled onto his back. The last sight he saw was more of the palace guards staring down at him.

Sinbad awoke with a start, mostly caused by a bucket of water being dumped upon his face. Angered, he was instantly on his feet, but a solid and powerful arm instantly pressed against his chest, stopping him where he stood.

"Hold Sinbad, they have Tishimi and the others." Sinbad looked up and saw Ralf's stoic face outlined in the dim light of the dungeon they both stood in. The guard who had thrown the bucket of water laughed maliciously then ordered them both to follow him.

"Where are the others?" Sinbad whispered.

"Safe." Replied Ralf in a low growl.

"No talking!" the guard barked.

Sinbad looked at the man's back angrily, imagining and wishing many evils upon him.

Sinbad, Ralf and the guard exited the dungeons and began climbing a circular steel staircase. Within minutes they entered an opulent room with many silk divans strewn about. Sinbad walked past scantily clad harem girls hidden behind silk shades. Many caught his eyes, and many smiled lustily at the mighty and handsome sailor.

Soon they entered another room, one filled with an even more opulent décor. Gold was embedded in everything and serving girl's filled gold chalices with wine for lounging royalty. Sinbad, Ralf and the guard were wholly ignored.

They passed through one more set of doors, these opened by powerfully built eunuchs.

Sinbad and Ralf, with their guard entered the chamber, the guard bowed low upon crossing the threshold. Within the chamber and standing nearby the caliph were Omar, Henri, Tishimi (Sans her precious blade), Haroun and Rafi. All seemed well enough and unharmed.

"Bow you dogs." hissed the guard.

Sinbad looked at him disdainfully, and then turned his gaze to the caliph. The man was sprawled upon his own silk divan like a bloated toad. Through thinly slit eyes he met Sinbad's gaze, "Do you not bow before your master? Do you not bow before the Caliph of Kahoun?"

"I do not recognize those who abduct me and my crew as our master." Sinbad crossed his chest and stared defiantly at the bloated toad who met his gaze incredulously.

The caliph pointed his finger at Sinbad and wagged it, while a great smile broke out upon his wide face, "You are insolent, I will grant you that O Sinbad the Sailor. That is one of the very reasons why I need you to serve me."

Sinbad stood unmoving, his arms still crossed upon his chest, "If you had need of our services, Caliph, you could have asked us as would any other client."

"Ah but Sinbad, you know as well as I, that I am not any other client. I am the caliph of Kahoun, and this day I require the services of the renowned Sinbad El Ari, the greatest sailor ever to cross the seven seas!"

Sinbad furrowed his brow, and tilted his head slightly, "For what purpose? You must know Caliph, you have lost much credibility with me for the way you abducted us all. You know my reputation as an honest sailor and businessman."

"Indeed I do, but I also know that no truly honest merchant sailor does business in Kahoun."

Sinbad relaxed marginally, "What do you wish of us, Caliph?"

"There is reputedly an island named Anarouch seven days journey west and south of here, have you heard of it?"

Sinbad cocked his head to the left and shook it, "Who hasn't? Most captains who know the name have brought their ships in search of it. It is, as legend would have it, a land of riches beyond measure. But how many times have each of us heard that before?"

The caliph looked about his great throne room, and then ordered his own guards, "Out you and you, all of you leave here now. I wish to speak with Captain Sinbad and his crew alone. Leave us." He clapped his hands and immediately al the guards left. Some stared suspiciously at Sinbad as they passed. The twin doors were reluctantly pulled shut behind them.

Once the Caliph was certain they were alone and none could hear him, he began to tell his tale, "Sinbad I need you to find that island. Something most precious to me is being held there, most precious indeed."

"What do you speak of, Caliph? There are riches within this room to fulfill any man's dreams."

"It is not riches, O Captain Sinbad. It is something worth far, far more. It is my daughter."

Sinbad gauged the countenance of the man before him then, and reluctantly found no deceit hidden there.

"What can we do to aid you Caliph? Why us? More so, how did your child come to be on that fabled island?"

The Caliph sighed, then turned and continued, "Two nights agone, a great roc flew into my daughters opened window, took her by the shoulders and flew away. The guards saw her being borne aloft and rightly decided not to loose arrows upon the giant bird, for fear of killing Yasmine. I rushed to her chambers when news of this dire evil had been passed to me. Once there I beheld a note left upon her bed by the monstrous bird. It read that all effort to rescue her would be met with abject and painful failure. It was signed by Abdul Bel-Fideel." the name hung in the air like a poison.

"The dreaded dark sorcerer?" Omar spat, "Allah have mercy on our souls."

Tishimi stared daggers of annoyance into the barrel chested first mates skull. Quickly Omar quieted down in response.

"Again I must ask, Caliph, why us? Many are the captains in your own fleet of vessels. Surely sending several of them would be sufficient to save your daughter the princess?"

"No, not a one is the equal of mighty Captain Sinbad. Your legend grows with each day alone. There is but one man I trust with the flower of my heart, Sinbad, and that is you. Only you have the resourcefulness and the temerity to save my child. There is no greater seaman anywhere upon the oceans."

"But I do not know where this accursed island is, no man does."

The caliph reached down and grasped a rolled up parchment near his own divan. He turned and tossed it to Sinbad. "These are directions to that thrice accursed place. My own sorcerer's and wizards performed great conjurings to discern Anarouch's true whereabouts. When you return with my daughter, I will fill your ship with riches the likes of which you have never before seen."

Sinbad laughed slightly, "I have seen quite a bit, Caliph. Trust in that."

"I do Captain Sinbad. That is why I need you, your crew and your ship. Only the great Captain Sinbad can find the Island of Anarouch and save my beloved Yasmine, I beg of you."

Sinbad looked at his crew. None seemed opposed to the idea, all nodded in agreement.

"What of this wizard you mentioned? How are we, mere merchant seaman to stand a chance of besting a black magician?"

"I will send my most powerful practitioner of magic in my employ with you. His name is Kaleel Al Suarazi. He practices white or good magic. He will aid your quest and will meet the dark wizard in battle if need be. He will also protect you from whatever magical entities Bel-Fideel may attack you with."

Sinbad looked to his crew once more, they all nodded, some reluctantly, but all were in agreement, "Very well, great Caliph. We will aid you, and when we return with your daughter, you will reward us with great riches. That is the bargain." Sinbad stuck his hand out, without hesitation the Caliph took it and shook it firmly.

That was six days ago. Now the Blue Nymph followed the map the Caliph had given them. With sextant and compass in hand, Sinbad stood upon the bow. Omar held the wheel in his steady and true hands, while up in the nest Haroun scanned the distance all about the Blue Nymph for some sign of the mysterious and dread Isle of Anarouch.

Sinbad stepped down, placing both feet upon the Blue Nymphs deck and walked with the steady stride of the accomplished seaman to Omar' side. He stared at his first mate silently for a moment. Omar finally turned and met his gaze, ""Go ahead you old lion. Tell me we were wrong to take this mission on."

Omar snorted derisively, "Why should I be made to tell you that which you already know, my Captain?"

Sinbad chuckled slightly, "You are as always ever to the point, my old friend."

"And yet still you do not heed my warnings. Even when they are unspoken still are you aware of them."

"Omar, there was naught I could have done. The Caliph would have insisted and perhaps resorted to force against us to do his bidding. This way when we are finished, at least we have full coffers."

Omar shrugged, "For a time anyway. I know you will find a way to spend every dinar that comes your way."

Sinbad smiled and clapped the stout first mate upon the back, "Ah you know me only too well my trusted friend, only too well."

Sinbad turned and walked toward Tishimi Osara. The female samurai sat with her back against the railing, sharpening her great katana. Sinbad sat beside her.

"You have been silent since we returned to the Blue Nymph. Why?"

"I should have killed them all when they boarded the Nymph." she replied angrily.

"Why did you not?"

"They held Haroun with a blade to his young throat. I did not wish for the boy to die."

"So then you did the correct thing Tishimi. Both of you are here now with us on yet another grand adventure instead of walking the lands of the dead."

She turned from her blade and looked Sinbad in the eyes, "I failed you. I will not do so again. You are my Captain and my leader. I have brought disgrace upon you."

Sinbad chuckled, "No Tishimi, you have brought great honor to me by staying alive and keeping my crew so as well. You and Haroun both are worth much more to me alive than dead. Without your great blade the coming battle will be that much more difficult."

Sinbad smiled and stood, walking away toward the below decks entry hatch.

Sinbad stepped down the staircase and entered the cabins. As it had been for days, the door to the cabin assigned to the wizard Kaleel Al Suarazi remained closed and locked. Sinbad paused but a moment as he raised his hand and hesitated to knock. Then he smiled slightly lowered his hand back to his side, and moved on.

There were few crewmen below decks, but most were topside. One of those below decks was the thin and white bearded Rafi. Sinbad knocked on his half open cabin door before entering. Rafi opened the door immediately, "My Captain! Welcome! Please, enter my humble cabin, please!" The man bowed low and backed up, allowing Sinbad egress.

"Stop that my friend. I need your insight not your fawning and platitudes."

Rafi shrugged and smiled, "Whatever you need, Captain, I am at your service."

"You are perhaps the most learned among the crew Rafi; do you think this mission is foolhardy? We travel into unknown seas with a wizard no one has seen since his first day aboard the Blue Nymph. We go against a mighty sorcerer and Allah only knows what else. Yes, I repopulated the crew with known warriors that the Caliph has lent us, but I do not know if I even trust them."

Rafi sat on the edge of his sleeping hammock and smiled a toothy grin, "Sinbad, you worry too much. We have faith in you, all of us do. You will see us through this adventure, as you always do. Why are you concerned? We have faced all kinds of deviltry before. Why are you concerned now? This is not the first time, nor do I believe it will be the last, that we will sail into unknown seas."

Sinbad grinned slightly before continuing, "My friend, something about all of this strikes me as...wrong. I do not trust the Caliph or the wizard he has sent us. Perhaps I am wrong, but the hackles on the back of my neck rise in warning at all of this."

"Sinbad, my Captain, all this poor learned healer can do is tell you that your instincts should never be ignored. Follow them when there is naught else to follow. They have never failed you before, they will not now."

Sinbad turned toward the door, smiling, "Thank you Rafi. Your advice as always is welcome and warranted."

Rafi bowed as Sinbad exited his room. The sailor began to walk toward his own large captain's quarters when he heard a commotion coming from above decks.

"What in the name of the profit?" Sinbad murmured as he stormed up the short staircase, taking two at a time.

He burst through the door to the deck and entered a seen of chaos and madness!

Bat winged creatures the size of young teenage boys with barbed tails and leathery skin were swooping out of the sky attacking his crew. They had faces like small alligators and short, stubby arms with razor sharp claws upon their hands.

Immediately Sinbad grabbed a scimitar from a fallen sailor's cold hand and attacked the nearest monster, slashing and hacking at its tough, thick skin.

"What are these devils? What hell did they escape from?" he bellowed to Omar.

"Only Allah knows Captain, and he is not speaking to me right now." Omar replied slashing for all his life against the monstrous foes attacking him.

"Where are they coming from?" Sinbad shouted.

An arrow flew by Sinbad's ear, so close he felt the air move at its passing. Turning his head, Sinbad saw Henri had crawled higher up the crow's nest rigging and was unleashing arrow after arrow from his fully packed quiver. Sinbad did not even turn his head to know that behind him lay a dead devil with an arrow threw its eye.

"Where is Gunarson?" Sinbad shouted.

"He must be below decks, perhaps he does not know of our predicament." Omar replied.

Sinbad hacked and slashed his way through what seemed like an almost endless wave of the dread monsters. Their claws hacked and slashed like razors and their teeth cut through skin and bone like papyrus. Blood covered the deck from a dozen dead or wounded crewmen.

Sinbad stabbed his sword through a creature's scaled neck, withdrawing it instantly to slash backward at the one standing nearest it. The pile of gore and serpent skinned bodies at his feet continued to grow.

But something garnered his attention he had seen moving out of the corner of his eye. It was Tishimi. She was moving in almost a blur. The female samurai was a fearless warrior, and this was her kind of fight. Hopeless odds, monstrous foes. She was in her element. She was also a thing of deadly beauty.

Tishimi Osara moved like a dancer, wielding her mystical katana with feline grace and controlled power. The monstrous foes were as nothing compared to her and her blade. She stepped over their reaching claws, and slashed a head from still twitching shoulders. Then she would duck low and avoid one that was flying toward her on its bat-like wings from behind. Slashing upward as it passed overhead, Tishimi split it in two and was covered head to toe in the thing's gore.

Sinbad attacked the nearest monster.

Her face now crimson with the blood of her enemies, Sinbad was certain he caught a smile upon her fair lips. A chill ran down his spine at the sight.

A ragged roar caught his attention as he condemned another of the beasts to a hell of its own choosing, for up from the decks below came an enraged, axe swinging berserker. Ralf, son of Gunar had joined the fray.

Bare skinned to the waist, his golden ponytail swinging behind him chaotically Gunarson was the antithesis of Tishimi. Where she was all grace and beauty with feline precision and agility, Ralf was almost a demon himself in battle. His double edged axe hummed as it split the air, slamming through monstrous heads and necks, as well as waists and legs. One beast sought to fly out of his reach, but with a berserker fury not known to the so-called civilized man, Ralf Gunarson grasped the creature by the leg and slammed it down to the deck splintering it with his ferocity alone. Howling like a wild beast, Gunarson lifted a discarded blade in his left hand and began hacking at multiple targets. He was almost akin to a force of nature. Raw, visceral, unstoppable.

"Sinbad! Look!" Haroun shrieked.

The mighty sailor turned his attention in the direction the boy had gesticulated to, and caught his breath in his mighty chest.

A creature sprang from the water, a long sinuous serpentine neck that wound up and up, with a massive head full of savage teeth at its end. Wings adorned the side of its head, as if they were ears.

"Oh this is wonderful." Omar grunted.

"Take heart good Omar, the day is not yet lost." Sinbad shouted as he ran toward the rear of the ship. Once there he ripped the canvas covering off of something he had installed on the Blue Nymph before they had left the port at Kahoun.

"By Odin's beard!" exclaimed Ralf, "You had a harpoon thrower installed."

The monster slammed its mouth into the deck, swallowing a sailor whole in one bite. The beast raised itself up toward the heavens again and let out an ear shattering roar that made everyone cover their ears instinctively.

Sinbad ignored his companions, save to shout, "Henri, I need you here. Keep the others away from me long enough to fire this thing."

"I am coming mon ami." Henri practically flew across the deck, avoiding the almost man-sized flying horrors while loosing arrow after arrow into others in his very path. He leaped and rolled dodging from one side to the other, more than once avoiding certain death in the form of the massive serpent slamming its jaws into the deck, seeking to take Henri in one bite whole.

The men that the Caliph had sent to join Sinbad's crew were able bodied warriors, but most had never seen the otherworldly. They were being killed quickly, leaving only the best of themselves alive and fighting back to back.

Sinbad turned the great harpoon and aimed it directly at the long twisting neck.

"Stay still, curse you." Sinbad muttered through grit teeth.

He fired the harpoon from its deck mounted gun. It flew straight and true through the air; embedding itself in the monsters neck halfway between the sea and its horrific head.

An ear splitting roar of agony spilled from the great beast's maw. It thrashed about savagely, slamming itself more than once into the deck of the Blue Nymph. The wooden deck and railing was turned to kindling. It slammed its terrible neck through the main sail tearing it asunder. Sailors leapt to and fro to avoid both the death throes of the serpent as well as the still attacking smaller monsters.

"Allah has once again abandoned us all, curse him." Omar breathed heavily, his endurance all but spent.

"Do not give up zee ship *Tu m'entends*! Fight on!" Henri shouted.

"We hear you, and I have no intention of giving up anything, let alone my beloved Blue Nymph." Sinbad replied.

The Serpent slammed into the deck one more bone jarring time, and then slid off of the deck slowly back into the briny deep from whence it came.

Nearby Tishimi stood shoulder to shoulder with Ralf and both were losing ground with each passing moment. Covered in gore, they appeared to be more demons from hell than warriors and heroes. But yet still they silently fought on.

Omar cursed loudly and fell over backward, a fanged monster instantly at his throat. The barrel chested first mate grasped the thing by its head and strained for all he was worth!

"Curse you Allah! Have I not always been a loyal son? Why do you bedevil me so?"

The creature dripped blood stained saliva all over Omar as it tried frantically to tear him apart. But with a recognizable twanging sound a handful of arrows appeared suddenly in the things back and neck. Omar kicked the lifeless corpse away with much effort and nodded his thanks to Henri, who quickly grasped a dangling line and swung across the deck, kicking two of the small monsters into the sea. He looked for all the world like the rogue he was. Henri landed next to Sinbad by the harpoon launcher.

Now all of the crew stood shoulder to shoulder near the harpoon launcher and fought together. Sinbad slashed madly at the tireless horrors that bit and clawed at them all. His black skin was covered in sweat and blood. His turban was long since gone, and his face and chest were streaked with blood. Some his own, some the monsters that continued to harangue them. Tishimi was silent death as her great blade sung a song that the creatures were beginning to fear. And Ralf, mighty Ralf was insane with red rage. His eyes wide and bloodshot, his great axe was once again held in two hands and split the air with savage rage. Henri ran out of arrows then and picked up a blade from a downed crewman. He began to hack and slash at the seemingly never ending creatures who continued to fly out of the sea and onto the deck.

Then, just when all was surely lost, the door to the companionway slammed open revealing a short turbaned figure with a full grey beard dressed in robes of red. His eyes blazed and his hands glowed, releasing blasts of fire that consumed the demon-things instantly while words in an unknown tongue sprang from his bearded lips.

All the hellish, bloodthirsty creatures were instantly immolated. Ash was all that remained of them.

Sinbad turned toward the small man, almost gasping from exhaustion, "Wizard, thank you for your aid. Without your help we would surely have died this day."

The wizard turned toward him, his dour countenance unreadable. Then after a short moment he turned and descended the steps to his quarters, once more locking the door from within.

Henri was the first to speak, "Why do I get the feeling I was just regarded as if I were but a lowly dog?"

"It is not you my friend," Sinbad somberly replied, "I felt the same disdain myself."

The next few hours were spent cleaning the deck of the Blue Nymph as well as burying the dead at sea.

The next morning found Sinbad and Omar staring over the rail at the open sea.

SINBAD and the Scorpion God

"Allah preserve us all, Sinbad," Omar started, "five crewmen went to their final resting place at sea."

"I know Omar. It will be that much more difficult for us all. They were friends and companions. They will be missed."

"What do we now, oh Captain?"

"We continue on, Omar. Our mission lies ahead of us. There is a young woman's life at stake, a princess."

"Not to mention untold riches eh?" Omar smirked.

"I know my friend, but you know as well as I the true reasons we do the things we do."

"Aye my Captain, for the adventure. We live to explore the unknown, and one day it may be the end of us all." Omar concluded with a shrug.

"Our fate is in Allah's hands." Sinbad nodded.

"I prefer that Thor lend me strength of arm to smite any foe that stands before me, for I send them to Valhalla in his honor."

Both men turned and watched a smiling Ralf approach.

Sinbad grinned, "You seem none the worse for wear this day?"

The big Norseman flexed his massive right bicep, "I feel fine, my companions. A night of bloodletting does wonders for my attitude the next morn."

He lifted his left arm up revealing a skin of wine, of which the blonde giant took a hearty pull from.

"So what Sinbad?" Ralf inquired.

Sinbad touched his neatly trimmed van dyke beard in thought for a moment, then smiled, "We continue on of course, after we affect repairs to the Blue Nymph. That sea monster did a large amount of damage, but thank Allah, none to our hull. Once those repairs are made to the best of our abilities we continue on."

"Should we find a nearby port and make our way there Captain?" Omar queried.

"There is no port for days in any direction and we are limping after the damage we took. But our hull is sound and our sails can be repaired aboard ship. For now the men can row. Once we arrive at the island of Anarouch some of the crew can remain behind to cut trees and make repairs while the rest of us search out the lost princess."

A female voice interrupted them, "She was not lost, she was taken."

The three men turned toward the voice and saw Tishimi approaching, and with her was Henri, his bow slung over his shoulder with a full quiver of arrows as well.

Sinbad nodded toward the quiver on his friends back and stated, "Are you expecting trouble?"

"Mon ami, after yesterday do you have to even ask?"

Sinbad chuckled, "No, I suppose not. In fact I applaud you for your diligence."

"You speak of my diligence, and yet your sword is slung across your back even while above decks. You are expecting more trouble as well."

"I am…cautious, Henri."

Omar harrumphed, "After yesterday, who can blame you, or any of us for being on edge?"

Sinbad stood, "In truth it is time we returned to working this ship. We will never arrive anywhere if we do not. Omar take command of your men. The rowers must begin. I will have some of the crew begin to stitch the main sail back together. "

Omar began shouting orders to the rest of the crew while the five companions went their separate ways about the ship.

Many leagues away, on the island of Anarouch, the evil wizard Abdul Bel-Fideel stared at the crystal ball before him. His fingertips caressed it while he murmured an incantation in a long forgotten tongue. The scene within the blood colored crystal was of the deck of the Blue Nymph itself. Abdul Bel-Fideel smiled, for he heard every word and saw what every man did upon the deck of the Blue Nymph.

"Why are you doing this, O evil magician? What do you plan for me? Speak to me, I am your captive, and can do you no harm, why do you ignore me?" a bound female, her arms held above her head by chains and her legs likewise tied to the ground cried out plaintively.

Finally Abdul Bel-Fideel turned to the girl. He was enwrapped in robes as black as the stygian depths. A turban of matching darkness adorned his head. In its center a blood-hued gem seemed to pulse with a life of its own. A sash the color of the very gem wrapped about his waist. He stood to full impressive height then, no longer leaning in closely to the crystal ball. His pointed van dyke beard seemed to quiver in anticipation.

"You would know why I took you from the only home, the only land you have ever known? Why it is simple O princess Yasmine; you are a virgin, and the blood of a royal virgin is a powerful thing. The blood of such a one can grant great powers to a knowledgeable sorcerer. It can grant immortality."

"You are mad." She whispered breathlessly.

"No my dear," He walked over and touched her below her chin, lifting her head of luxurious brown hair so that he could stare her in her beautiful grey eyes, "I am destined. When I sacrifice you, I will gain enough power to rule over all of the known world."

"No…" she pulled away from his touch, repulsed by it, "My father will save me. He will never stop trying to rescue me. Even if you…murder me," the words caught in her tender throat, "he will still make you pay."

"Hahaha, you put too much faith in your father, child." Abdul Bel-Fideel walked away from the princess, and returned to his crystal ball, "Even now he sends a ship after me, how the fool found this island I know not, but he sends the mighty Captain Sinbad after me, and he is mighty indeed. His bourgeoning legend does him well, I must tell you. I sent a monster from the deep and all its scaled children to destroy him and sink his precious Blue Nymph to the oceans depths, and yet somehow the sailor defeated them all. Furthermore, some charm must have been laid upon them all for I could not see the events as they transpired. This will be perhaps more entertaining than I originally supposed, but only time will truly tell."

The girl in her fine silks with her bare midriff spat at him, "You are a devil, a monster!"

"You are mistaken my dear, devils and monsters work for me, I am something far, far worse."

Sinbad stood at the wheel, holding a steady and true course. Every so often he would turn to Haroun in the crow's nest and the boy would shake his head negatively, a sadness writ about his suntanned face.

Sinbad sighed. The attack on the ship had taken its toll on them all. The crew was beginning to grumble. They had yet more than enough provisions onboard for many more weeks of travel, but still, twas not a good sign that they were at sea now nine days for a journey that was rumored to take only seven.

"Omar, come here." Sinbad commanded.

Omar had just exited the cabin area and the section of the ship that housed the oars and rowing benches.

"What is it my Captain?" the barrel-chested man replied.

"Hold the wheel. I think it is time I spoke to our unsociable guest."

"Do you believe that is wise sahib? The wizard shot flames from his hands and burned hell spawned devils to ash."

"Aye my friend, but since I am neither hell spawn nor devil I believe I will be safe. Besides he is a guest upon my ship, in truth my home. It is time he began to act like a proper guest and not one who considers himself above those he travels with."

"May Allah protect you."

Sinbad smiled and nodded his thanks, then turned and exited the deck, heading down to the cabin area.

A minute later he stood before the door of the wizard. He raised his hand to knock and the door slowly swung open before he could touch it.

"Enter." A deep and powerful voice ordered.

Sinbad immediately bristled at this. But enter he did.

Walking purposely forward into the midst of the cabin he stopped as soon as he came upon the wizards sleeping area. His eyes widened in disbelief at what he saw. For here was the white bearded wizard sitting on cushions floating in the air five feet above the floor.

The wizard again looked down upon him coldly, "What is it Captain Sinbad?"

Sinbad met his steely gaze with one of his own, "I have come to ask what you are doing in this room for the past nine days. The only time anyone has seen you was during the attack."

"Yes, the attack I saved you all from if I recall, correct?"

"Yes, you did. You have my thanks for that as well, but that is not the reason I am here."

"Oh? Then what is?"

"I wish to know what you can do to get us to our destination faster."

The wizard stuck a single digit into the air pointing upward, "Ah, you seek my aid in arriving at the island of Anarouch."

Sinbad crossed his arms upon his mighty chest, "I do, wizard. The faster we arrive at that accursed place the faster this madness can be done with."

"Ah," the wizard hissed, "You grow tired of this journey and are unsure of where you go."

Sinbad chortled, "Do not flatter yourself Kaleel Al-Suarazi, I know exactly where we go and in what direction. But somehow the voyage is taking us longer than anticipated."

"I see. You believe that Abdul Bel-Fideel may have cursed our journey."

Sinbad nodded, "I do. There can be no other explanation for it. The devil has hexed us all."

Calm yourself Captain Sinbad, I will look into this. If there is any truth to it, you will know immediately. In the meantime I will see what I can do to speed along our voyage. Would that aid you?"

Sinbad nodded grimly, "It would Kaleel Al-Suarazi."

"Very well Captain, now please, I ask that you allow me to continue my meditations. We go to face a powerful enemy in Abdul Bel-Fideel. I must continue to meditate if I am to be powerful enough to stand against that devil."

Sinbad's spine went cold at this, "What do you say? Is he not a man?"

"Sadly Captain Sinbad, he is far less than a man and perhaps far more."

"You speak in riddles, wizard."

"My kind always does Sinbad El Ari; it is our nature to do so. This man we go to face is evil and foul. Be aware that any and every advantage must be taken against him. Now leave. I must continue to meditate. I now prepare to face the battle of my life against a foe that makes concessions with demons."

"Do not all you sorcerer's deal with devils?"

The wizard looked down upon Sinbad from his floating perch disdainfully, "No Sinbad, though you may think all magicians are evil men, I myself and others of my order are men of pure hearts and souls. We seek to do good in the world and to stave off the forces of the darkness that devils like Abdul Bel-Fideel embrace."

Sinbad nodded slowly, "Very well Kaleel Al-Suarazi. I will summon you when we arrive at the dreaded island of Anarouch."

"Do not bother Captain, for I will be aware of our arrival before your man in the crow's nest."

Sinbad nodded, "Very well. If you require refreshment or food call and your needs will be met."

"I require naught for now, sir, save my solitude."

Sinbad exited the room and shut the door behind him without a word more.

'Wizards and devils. No matter how many times I come upon the two I am no more used to their presence than the time before. Ever am I a simple son of the sea. There are some things men should not be made to deal with. Dark sorcery, hell, sorcery of any kind is surely the worst of those things.' Sinbad mused to himself.

He exited the cabin area and reappeared on the top deck. Immediately he recognized that the ship was moving faster with a strong wind behind it now, where earlier there had been none.

"Omar, where did this blow come from? There was barely any breeze when I went below decks."

The stout smaller man shook his head slowly, "I know not Captain. There was no warning of it, and it moves us without our main sail. It is as if the ocean has taken us in the palm of its hand and now speeds us along toward our very destination. Surely it is magic."

Sinbad smiled at his friend and first mate, remembering his conversation with the wizard scant moments ago "You are correct Omar, magic it is indeed."

Sinbad clapped Omar on the shoulder then made off toward a relaxed Henri Delacrois who was sitting in the net, sharpening his arrowheads.

"You are well Henri?"

The smaller man nodded and smiled slightly, "Oui mon Capitaine. I merely ready my arrows for their next need."

"Good. You did well yesterday you know."

Henri smiled, "Surely mon ami, you did not expect less of Henri the Gaul, did you?"

Sinbad chuckled, for he was always a man of good humor, even in the face of battle and the unknown, "No my friend, I expect only the best of the finest crew to sail the seven seas. Yesterday you all delivered. But what I fear is what lies ahead of us all."

"You believe there to be more deviltry in wait for us upon that island?"

"Worse my friend. I believe we will encounter it before we ever arrive there."

Henri nodded grimly, "Very well. I will surely make more arrows before we arrive, and I will make sure they are sharp enough to shave with."

"As long as it is a very close shave then I will be pleased with the result."

"But of course Capitaine, only the best for you, oui?"

"It is what I demand from my crew Henri, as you well know."

Sinbad turned and walked away.

The Blue Nymph sped along over the water, as if it had a full tail wind. Yet the sail was destroyed and not mended yet. But still she flew across the placid sea.

Sinbad returned to Omar's side and took the wheel from him. The stout first mate stared at Sinbad's troubled countenance a moment before finally speaking, "What troubles you sahib?"

"That wizard below deck. He claims to be on our side, to fight for the good of the Caliph as well as this ship, but I do not trust him."

Omar shrugged, "Since when is that something new? It is a wizard. They are not to be trusted and their ways are impossible to understand."

"This I know my friend. But that does not mean that I have to like it, or trust our mysterious friend."

"My Captain, trust in your instincts as you well know, they have not failed us yet."

Sinbad smiled, "Your council is indeed worthy as always, Omar."

"Do not be fooled Sinbad, I do not trust magicians either, especially ones who skulk in shadow and out of reach of the glorious sun. Also, I do not like that this wizard can so control the elements that he makes a sail-less ship skip across the waves at a speed greater than it has ever achieved."

"Aye Omar, in that we both agree, but to be honest my friend, I asked him to do so."

"So he was following your commands in this?"

Sinbad stoically nodded in the affirmative.

"Well perhaps then he is not all bad, eh?" Omar grinned, which for him was a rare thing.

"Perhaps, Omar, but still do I not trust this man. Also I do not like the way he...dismissed me. This is my ship, not his. I have had difficult passengers before, but never one who perceived himself as master of this vessel."

"Is that what you feel this wizard is doing?" Omar asked with widened eyes.

"I do Omar. That is what I am sensing."

The older man whipped his scimitar off of his hip and brandished it in the air. "Then perhaps I will pay a visit to him and cut the cur down to size."

Sinbad laughed, "You over-react my old friend. While I felt no overt threat toward us from this man, what I felt was...condescension."

"The dog looked down upon you?"

"Aye that is what I felt. But in truth as I have already mentioned, I felt no threat from the man." Sinbad looked about the speeding Blue Nymph.

"Land ho!" Haroun shouted from the crow's nest.

Sinbad handed the wheel back to Omar and without a word bounded up the net toward the nest, stopping just below it, he stared in the direction that Haroun was pointing.

Sinbad smiled, "Good job boy, good job." Sinbad smiled at his lookout, and scampered down the net as sure footedly as if he were walking upon the streets of Baghdad.

"Follow the boy's direction, Omar. The mysterious isle of Anarouch is ahead!"

"I will…cut the cur down to size."

Sometime later...

The Blue Nymph was anchored off of the island of Anarouch. Two small boats were rowed ashore and run up upon the sandy and rock strewn beach. Men gathered driftwood and started fires near the boats. Sinbad, Haroun, Ralf, Rafi, Tishimi, Henri and the wizard Kaleel Al-Suarazi were gathered by one fire, the rest of the crew that came ashore by another. Omar stayed aboard the Blue Nymph with the majority of the crewmen.

"You truly believe we are safe here upon this beach Sinbad?" Haroun asked, his mop of dark hair bouncing up and down as he spoke.

"For now yes. I do not fear this place so close to the beach. You all keep your swords at the ready tonight. A two man watch will be kept near each campfire and shifts will rotate every two hours. At first light we head into the jungle."

"Why are we not sleeping tonight in the Blue Nymph instead of on this beach?" Haroun continued.

"Because Haroun, I want everyone to have their land legs under them when we begin to explore this place. I do not know how far we will have to travel until we can find that accursed sorcerer and the Princess Yasmine. Best for everyone's legs to be used to dry land before we start. There may be accursed things hiding beyond the jungle's edge waiting to attack us. I'd rather force them to come to the beach instead of us going to them."

"Nothing will attempt to attack us this night, I have taken precautions." the scarlet garbed wizard offered, "We will all be safe. Come the morning though will be a different concern."

"I thought you magicians preferred the night?" Haroun asked.

"No boy, that is a foolish fairy tale. Especially for one such as myself who practices white or good magic."

"Many pardons." Haroun bowed.

"No offense was taken, boy. But in the morning at dawns light we will have the forces of a powerful wizard allied against us. Get rest this night, for tomorrow you may need it."

The wizard rolled over without another word upon his sleeping mat and fell asleep.

Sinbad shrugged, and then clapped his hands, "Put down your wine skins. It is time we slept as well. If the wizard is correct tomorrow will be a day we won't soon forget."

In the jungle, just beyond the tree line, red eyes watched malevolently.

Morning came too quickly, with Sinbad being the first to wake. Walking from sleeping mat to sleeping mat he called, "Up you men, tis time to explore this strange new land. Adventure and destiny awaits. Up, up I say!"

Groggily the crew began to rouse from their sleep. Within minutes they were all standing and ready to enter the jungle proper.

Tishimi stood near an overgrown jungle path. Sinbad approached her, "What is it Tishimi? You stare down that trail as if the devil himself awaits at the end of it."

"Perhaps he does Sinbad. Something is not right there. I can just…feel it."

"Harrumph. I will never doubt your instincts, samurai. We will be cautious." he replied with a wink.

Tishimi began to walk into the somewhat obscured path into the teeming jungle when a mad figured hurled itself at her from deep within the brush!

"What?" She managed to get out before she was bowled over by a charging madman! Naked to the waist, a veritable mane of wild black hair with a thick, unkempt beard; the lunatic exploded out of the woods, knocking over Tishimi, actually running through her. If she had drawn her katana, he would have been split in two.

The madman shoved Tishimi to the ground and then ran straight into Sinbad's fist.

"Down you dog!" the enraged captain roared, "You are lucky Tishimi did not slaughter you on the spot."

The filthy, unkempt man lay on the ground gibbering madly.

Henri reached Tishimi first and offered his hand to help her up. But the proud warrior merely brushed him off and stood on her own.

"Are you well Tishimi?" Sinbad asked.

"I am fine, Sinbad. I saw this madman coming at me and did not want to murder him on the spot."

"I understand proud warrior. You performed well as always, in service of your Captain and crew."

She bowed, "My sword is yours to command."

Ralf Gunarson grabbed the crazed stranger by the neck and raised him upright, "You, dog! Where do you come from?" the ponytailed Norseman bellowed, "What do you here?"

The man who was of the same height as Sinbad squirmed in the warriors grip, then choked, "Let-me-go!"

He spun and kicked Ralf in the groin. The big warrior dropped him and doubled over. But he was almost instantly back up and charging after the wild man. An all-consuming rage turned his eyes red with anger. Within three steps he had caught the fleeing man, grabbed him by his filthy head of hair, lifted him up and hurled him to the ground at Sinbad's feet.

The nearly naked man lay there whimpering. Sinbad knelt down, "Do not rise again my friend. I would hate for one of my people to hurt you in some way."

The man lifted his head up and looked at Sinbad, a certain clearness of mind and thought began to show in his eyes.

"What are you doing here, mad one? How long have you been here? What are you called?"

"I am Adorno." The man replied gutturally.

"Why are you here Adorno?"

"I-I was shipwrecked here, then taken captive by the mad sorcerer...I-I Where am I? Who are you people?" he murmured.

"Here, let me have a look at him." Rafi the Greek medicine man spoke.

Quietly and gently Rafi looked over Adorno, slowly moving him side to side and examining him from the bottom of his feet to the top of his head.

"He is malnourished, but that is readily apparent. He is not dehydrated, though."

Sinbad somberly nodded his approval, "That is a good thing, Rafi."

"How so?" the Greek trained physician asked without looking up.

"For it means there is fresh water upon this isle, and that it has not been poisoned. We can fill our casks from this body of water as well as our skins. The Blue Nymph's water supply will be replenished."

The man called Adorno still lay there quivering on the sand when Sinbad returned his attention to him.

"Why were you running out of the jungle Adorno? Was something chasing you?"

Adorno shook his head quickly and seemingly non-stop until Sinbad put a hand to his shoulder.

"What was it, man? What was chasing you that could instill such fear in you?"

The drooling, shaking man looked past Sinbad, over his shoulder and began to point a wavering hand to a point further down the beach.

All the hands turned as one, and as one their hearts froze in their breasts. For coming toward them were two horrific looking creatures. Giants, complete with clubs in their hands. They stood at least thirty feet tall, taking huge steps that swallowed distance.

"Quickly", Haroun shouted, "back to the ship!"

"There is no time Haroun. We must make our stand here." Sinbad ordered. His scimitar hissed from its scabbard. An instant later Tishimi's katana was released from her own. The rest of the men joined up beside them. Ralf stood next to Sinbad, with Henri standing next to Tishimi, his bow already in his hands with an arrow nocked. Gunarson swung his axe slowly from side to side with vehement disdain for the towering monsters that continued to advance upon them all.

"Halt you giants. Turn around now and your lives will be spared, you have the word of Captain Sinbad."

"Your word matters not to us." one giant rumbled, "We will kill you all and feast on your flesh."

"Now there is a cheery thought." Henri opined.

Sinbad looked to his marksman; "Henri." is all he said. Henri nodded, and loosed arrow after arrow into the two behemoths.

But the giants merely plucked the arrows from their thick leather vests and laughed heartily. They continued to advance.

"That is not confidence inspiring." Henri muttered.

"Aim for their eyes." Sinbad hissed.

Henri nodded and let loose a volley of arrows hither to undreamed of by the giants.

Instinctively the two monstrosities covered their eyes. Other crewmen now released volley after volley of arrows. Henri may have been the most proficient with his favorite weapon, but there were others amongst the crew who knew how to shoot adequately enough on their own.

Ten men took to releasing countless arrows at the behemoths, who tentatively covered their eyes and began stepping backward.

That was enough for Gunarson. With a maddened roar he hurled himself toward the giants, Tishimi and a few other brave souls only a few steps behind him. Gunarson began hacking at the closest giant's ankle.

With a maddened roar the giant tried to smack Ralf from his ankle, but the big Norseman ducked low, the giant's hand skimming over his head.

Tishimi ran to the other leg and stabbed it through with her sword.

"Archers, continue to harangue them." bellowed Sinbad.

Now he ran to the attack himself joining Tishimi and Ralf on the nearer giant. The one a step behind his nearly overcome brother was faring no better. Arrows continued to fly for his eyes. His arm was bristled with arrows, each one biting deep into unprotected flesh.

The crewmen were close to each of his legs stabbing and jabbing repeatedly.

"I'll crush you all!" the rearward giant roared angrily. It lifted its foot and slammed it down, crushing a half dozen seamen. Haroun himself was almost killed if not for his quick reflexes.

"See? I kill many with one step of my foot. Now we will crush the rest of you all."

"Retreat from his ankle." Sinbad shouted.

But the giant kicked this time, sending bodies high into the air, to land with bone shattering finality upon the rock strewn beach.

"We are running out of arrows." Henri wailed.

"Fall back!" Sinbad repeated. He reached up and grabbed Ralf by the shoulder forcibly turning him.

"Raarrrr!" Gunarson snarled madly, his Norse features twisted madly.

"Snap out of it warrior, follow me, we must get away from these things. Come quickly."

Ralf shook his head and his mind seemed to clear. Turning he ran behind Sinbad and Tishimi, realizing that to die this day would do no one any good.

"Where do we run to? Any moment those…monsters will overtake us all." Tishimi stated.

"The boats. Get to the boats. Once on the water we may have a chance." Sinbad shouted.

Already those closest to the two boats were shoving them back into the surf as quickly as possible. Behind the running crew the giants thundered along the beach.

"Odin's eye!" swore Ralf, "each step they make sounds like Thor's own thunder."

"They are making plenty of steps." replied Haroun.

The crew ran for the boats and were pulled aboard by those already within them.

"Row you dogs, row!" commanded Sinbad. He grabbed a bow and quiver from one of his men who was rowing and begin firing arrow after arrow along with Henri into the towering enemies.

"Mon Dieu!" exclaimed Henri, "they continue to chase us into the very water!"

"I know, it is what I was hoping for." Sinbad growled.

His crew all turned to look at him in astonishment.

"Do not look at me, put your backs into it, hurry, our survival depends on it."

The men redoubled their efforts. The giants were walking toward them, their chests still above the water line, when with a loud twang a missile shot from the Blue Nymph, and embedded itself in the closer giant's throat!

"The harpoon?" Rafi exclaimed.

"Aye. I left instructions with Omar to have the harpoon manned at all times, and if they saw us being chased back to the ship by something monstrous to use it."

"Well this certainly counts." Haroun agreed.

"Only one is downed though the second is still coming." Tishimi calmly recognized.

"It is gaining on us." Ralf grunted. He stood and brandished his mighty axe.

"It will take Omar and the men some minutes to reload the harpoon." Sinbad growled.

"Allah protect us, we are lost." Haroun cried.

"No." Ralf roared, "Odin guide my hand!" Without hesitation Ralf hurled his axe at the quickly closing giant. Its head was barely above the water line now, and the axe embedded itself with a deafening 'thwack' right between the terrible creature's eyes. The axe went in deep, almost to the handle.

At first the giant continued to walk, placing one lumbering foot in front of the other. But then its eyes rolled up in its head, its mouth sagged open, and the giant fell over backward beneath the waves. Only a bit of its forehead and the axe handle itself remained above the water. Ralf jumped into the water, swam over to the dead giant's carcass and with an animal-like roar tore the axe free.

Ralf swam the short distance back to the boat and climbed in. Sinbad helped pull him aboard.

"That was incredible!" the wide eyed Haroun gushed.

Ralf only shrugged while wiping his blade clean, "It was his skull or our lives. There was no real choice there, boy."

"Now what, Sinbad?" Tishimi asked.

"Now we re-supply and return to that accursed island."

Sinbad turned about quickly then, looking from boat to boat, "Where is that damned wizard of ours? Was he killed on the shore? In fact, where is the madman from the jungle?"

"I have seen neither since the giants appeared upon the beach," Henri replied, "I do not believe they were killed, but they seem to have both disappeared."

"Allah preserve us all." Sinbad grumbled.

"So then where are they both?" Ralf growled.

"Walk you, haggard excuse for a man." Kaleel Al-Suarazi prodded, "return me to whence you escaped from your master."

"N-no. H-he will k-kill me for escaping him."

"And I will kill you if you do not bring me to him, you fool. Besides, I come to kill this bastard sorcerer. Stay behind me once we begin to do battle and you will survive. I cannot help you if you run."

"Y-you would help me?"

"You have some worth Adorno. You know this island and of the accursed idiot who runs it. When we get to him, you will fall in behind me."

Adorno bowed his head, looking at his filthy feet, "Y-yes m-my master."

Kaleel Al-Suarazi nodded and smiled contentedly. Then with the end of a gnarled branch he had picked up along the way and was using as a walking stick, he prodded Adorno along.

An hour and a half later the two small boats ran up the beach once more.

"Secure your anchors in the sand. We do not want high tide to wash the boats away," Sinbad ordered, "It is a long swim back to the Blue Nymph otherwise."

"Yes Captain Sinbad." A sailor named Jamal answered.

"You took much more of the crew with us this time my Captain. Why?" Tishimi asked.

"You are a warrior Tishimi, why do you think? Twenty men I did take with us this time to the beach, and only two will remain with the boats. We will storm this island with eighteen strong. That may be nothing in man power, but wizards are an odd lot. My belief is that he will have very few men with him. In fact it may be him alone or other poor souls like that Adorno who ran into us."

"Ah but what of our wizard? He is gone now too, with the madman Adorno."

"That man was never 'our wizard', Tishimi. He but traveled with us, but his agenda was ever his own. Since he has left us without a word, I am glad I questioned that agenda and kept a close eye on him while onboard the Blue Nymph."

"So what now?" Henri joined them and asked.

"Now we forge ahead through the jungle and find this Abdul Bel-Fideel, as well as the princess Yasmine."

"Up you men," called Ralf the Norseman, "our journey through this jungle is about to begin."

The crewmen rose from the beach where they had sat awaiting the order to move out and began to filter into the jungle on the barely visible path.

At the head of the line was Sinbad himself along with Tishimi and Henri, who led the way. His tracking skills were second to none, but Sinbad and Tishimi were both experienced trackers as well.

"There is a trail this way. It is faint but they passed this way only a few short hours ago." Henri advised.

"Agreed Henri, I see it as well." Sinbad agreed.

"As do I." Tishimi confirmed.

The eighteen men continued on, walking through the stinking jungle for hours, knowing they were still sometime behind their quarry.

"Sinbad," Henri called, "there is a clearing up ahead."

Sinbad nodded his turbaned head slowly, "Tread carefully my friend. I have no doubt this is a trap."

Henri nodded in agreement, and tentatively entered the clearing, his sword at the ready. While Henri was a master with a bow, he was only mediocre with a blade. But that being said, his skills had never failed him yet.

Slowly he crept into the circular clearing, staying close to its edges. Sinbad, Tishimi and Ralf followed him in, with the rest of the men behind them.

It was then that the center of the clearing exploded upward revealing half a dozen twelve foot long cobra's standing on their tails, towering above the surprised crew.

"Swords out, defend yourselves!" shouted Sinbad.

The serpents dove in, looking to kill the invaders quickly and with a cunning intelligence.

Ralf left his axe hanging at his waist and used his broadsword instead. Wider and heavier by far than the slim scimitars the rest of the crew used, his blade was still a deadly blur. His first attack lopped the head off of the serpent nearest to him. "One is down." he shouted.

Tishimi matched moves with a darting serpent. It hissed and stabbed at her, but her blade was a deadly thing, seemingly moving of its own accord at times, and perhaps it was, for according to Tishimi's own tale the spirit of her father, the master sword-smith, resided within the blade.

"Father guide my hand." she hissed, her own words matching the sibilant sounds of the coiling horrors.

Again and again the snakes struck, trying to kill the sailors with each lightning fast attack. Again and again the crew parried and struck back.

"This is madness," shouted Henri.

"What is wrong, Gaul?" Ralf asked.

"I hate snakes you fool, they…unnerve me."

"Ha ha, here little man, let me get that for you." Ralf's sword slashed out and split another cobra in two.

"Aaaaaa!" One of the crew screamed, his red sash swirling about him. All heads turned to him but it was too late. The last cobra crawled away from the convulsing man.

"Bastard!" Sinbad shouted. His blade lashed out like a serpent itself, slaying the snake instantly.

Rafi, the Greek medic trained shipmate ran over to the seaman, who was convulsing and foaming at the mouth. Within seconds he convulsed no more.

Rafi turned toward Sinbad sadly and shook his head.

Sinbad turned angrily, "This Abdul Bel-Fideel has more to answer for now. I swear to you all I will be the one to ask the final question."

Sinbad El-Ari turned and stormed off down the end of the path out of the clearing. Anger was clouding his eyes, but not his judgment. He quickly surveyed the ground before him and avoided any last traps left in their path.

Moments later they all entered into a vast sandy clearing, and at its center sat a palace worthy of the greatest sultan. It gleamed golden in the sunlight sparkling so brightly as to be almost blinding.

"This is madness." Ralf grunted.

"No," growled the maddened Sinbad, "this is sorcery."

"But still there is no sign of Kaleel Al-Suarazi, or the wild man Adorno." noticed Haroun.

"No, not yet, but their tracks lead to this spot before disappearing. They must be inside."

The group of sailors headed cautiously toward the doors of the towering palace.

They approached within a dozen feet of the gilded steps leading to the doors when the twin doors were hurled open from within. Out walked a dozen golden suits of armor, each one was brandishing a blade in its metallic fist.

"L-look at their faces!" Haroun pointed.

Sinbad's eyes followed Haroun's finger and he stopped in his tracks. A chill ran up his back. He spoke one word in a low, hushed growl, "Sorcery."

Swords out, defend yourselves!" Sinbad shouted.

For the helmets were over empty skulls! The armored suits housed skeletons that now quickly moved to the attack.

Sinbad himself led the charge, attacking madly, his blade a flashing thing.

"You hell spawned dogs will not stave our mission."

Tishimi and Ralf were on either side of him, Haroun next to Ralf. Henri stood back slightly and let arrows fly in quick succession. Each one unerringly finding chinks in the gleaming armor, but to no avail. The skeletal warriors continued marching toward them and attacking.

"Sinbad," Henri called, "my arrows are not working. It is as if when they strike, nothing is there."

"Then draw your sword." Sinbad shouted, all the while his sword clanged again and again against one of the skeletal warriors.

"Draw my sword? Do you want me to die?" Henri replied nervously.

"It does not matter how weak your swordsmanship is, it will avail us all better than your arrows are at the moment." Tishimi shouted.

Sinbad ducked below a swinging golden blade then hacked at the knee of the horrific warrior he was fighting. The skeleton crumpled, its lower leg broke off and shot out from under it skittering away across the sand filled clearing.

Sinbad brought his scimitar down hard upon its skinless neck, shattering the armor. Then with a powerful kick he sent the decapitated head spinning into the air. The rest of the armor fell to the ground with a clank and lie there unmoving.

"The head is their weakness, remove the head." Sinbad roared.

His men far outnumbered the ghastly skeletons, but still were they hard pressed. Sword was driven against sword amid huffing men and eerily silent skeletons, the only sound they made was the metallic clamor of their armor or the din of sword meeting sword.

"Sinbad, their strength…" howled one of the crew.

"I know Abdul, these monsters are supernaturally strong." Sinbad replied.

Tishimi made a quick two stroke attack, her blade passing through the suit of armor where a man's heart would be. The enemy she battled convulsed once and fell to the ground shattering into pieces.

"Tishimi's blade, its magic is repellent to the creatures." Gunarson shouted.

"Aye it is indeed," Sinbad agreed, "Form around her those of you who are not as skilled as some others.

"Bah, I need no one's protection." Ralf Gunarson roared. He began to whirl his massive axe above his head, his pony tail actually spinning behind him, mimicking his movements. Then with a roar that shook everyone to their cores he waded into the skeletons lopping off head after head.

Tishimi quietly continued her attacks, driving her blade through leering skulls, instantly returning the animated skeletons to death.

Sinbad himself stabbed his sword through a skull's jaw and out the back of its helmet. With a twist he snapped the head off at the neck and flung the helmet and skull away.

A bellow of agony rang out and all turned toward it. One of the crewmen, Agnar by name, was run through by a grinning skeleton. Lifeless, he fell off the blade, almost instantly surrounded by a quickly growing pool of his own blood.

Sinbad raised his scimitar up in rage about to charge the undead creature when a bow twanged repeatedly. Five arrows embedded themselves in the skeletons leering maw before the empty skull finally broke off and fell to the ground, followed immediately by the rest of the body. Everyone turned in the direction the arrows had come from to see Henri lowering his bow.

He shrugged, "We found their weak spot."

The raiding party cautiously entered the doors of the palace, one worthy of a maharajah himself. It was magnificent. The foyer was thirty feet high, with gilded staircases winding up to unknown rooms.

But Sinbad led his crew down instead, choosing equally winding stairs that reached downward to untold depths.

Once they entered the doorway that led below the stately palace the group immediately came upon lit torches in sconces along the wall. Sinbad had taken one and every second man in the group grabbed one as well. Eight lit torches, sixteen sailors. They stepped down a long and winding stair case that disappeared in the darkness beneath the palace.

Sinbad turned to Rafi, "Stay here my friend. What lies below is battle and battle only. Guard our way out of this hellish place."

Rafi nodded and gripped the hilt of his own sword in its scabbard, "I will, my Captain."

Sinbad clapped him on the shoulder and began descending the winding stone steps.

"I cannot see." Henri muttered.

"None of us can. This staircase is unnaturally dark." Sinbad hissed in reply. "Continue down it. Our enemy must await at the bottom."

"Sinbad," Tishimi whispered, "Do you hear something?"

Sinbad strained his ears, and peered over the edge of the roughhewn stone staircase they were working their way down.

Now Sinbad heard faint sounds wafting up to greet them. They were the sounds of men fighting and arguing.

The steps were cut around the tunnel that went straight down in a circular pattern.

"What man could have cut these steps so far down that I cannot see their end? Do we descend into hell itself?" Sinbad asked aloud.

No one answered him.

The group moved down and down into the unfathomable darkness, penetrated only by their dimly burning torches. Tishimi looked at Sinbad's sash and frowned, "Sinbad," she whispered, "that damnable blade is back."

Sinbad looked at his sash and saw the hilt of the dagger called 'Grachene' protruding there.

"The damned thing has returned yet again, Tishimi. It must sense blood to be spilled."

"Well of that Grachene and I are of the same mind at least." The samurai warrior women nodded gravely.

Sinbad felt the weight of the blade in his sash with mixed emotions. He hated the thing, its mystic origins in the underworld of Queen Persephone never sat right with the sailor. But he knew against mystic foes it would come in handy.

After many minutes the group came to the end of the stone staircase. They found a flat floor lit by torches and nothing more.

Henri looked up toward the top of the stone steps somewhere high above, "Mon Dieu, we must surely be in the devil's own hell to have descended so far."

Ralf grunted, "Huh. If this be Hel I welcome it for if your devil does indeed dwell here, he has much to answer for from me. I look forward to splitting him in two." Ralf hefted his axe mightily.

"Allah preserve us." Sinbad sighed. He began walking into an adjoining tunnel before them, leading his group of adventurers into darkness.

"I do not like this place." Tishimi breathed restlessly.

"You are always a bit claustrophobic, non?" Henri asked.

"I fear nothing." She hissed in reply.

"Both of you quiet down." Sinbad ordered. "There are voices ahead."

They stepped cautiously to the end of the tunnel they had just traversed. With a raised hand Sinbad stopped them all so that they were still hidden in shadow.

"What is it?" Tishimi hissed.

"Look for yourselves, but carefully."

One at a time Tishimi, Rolf and Henri peered ahead and then stopped, cautiously stepping back.

"It is Abdul Bel-Fideel and Kaleel El-Suarazi. They are doing mystic battle with one another. The wretch named Adorno is on his hands and knees quaking in fear in the corner. The room is a temple of some kind." Sinbad explained to the rest.

"But what kind of temple?" a sailor named Ahmad asked.

"There is a giant statue made of gold of a scorpion at its center. It is some kind of Scorpion god." Sinbad replied.

"What kind of accursed thing is that?" breathed Hanoud.

"I fear we are about to find out." Sinbad answered.

They continued to look on as the two sorcerers battled. Lightning was thrown from the fingertips of one at the other, who replied with blasts of flame to his enemy. Thunder and fury rocked the temple with deafening intensity. The pyrotechnics they blasted each other with were eye searing in brightness.

But it became readily apparent that Kaleel Al-Suarazi was losing. Moment by moment he was receiving the worst of the attacks, not giving them.

"Aaaa!" screamed Al-Suarazi, as his flesh burned, blistering instantly under Abdul Bel-Fideel's attack.

"Look!" Pointed Henri with a hiss, for there on the altar, underneath the towering golden statue of the scorpion lie a bound and gagged Princess Yasmine. She stared upward wide eyed and fearful at the giant golden scorpion above her. If not for the gag in her mouth she would have been screaming. Her eyes were tear filled. Her head hung off the altar and her long brown hair streamed to the ground beneath her.

"What do we do?" Tishimi asked.

"We can waste no more time. If Kaleel Al-Suarazi does not turn the tide, he as well as we may be doomed. We must aid him and save the princess. Tishimi, Rolf and Henri, you are with me. Haroun you take the rest of the men and cut the girl free." Sinbad commanded.

The group cut into two and began their attacks.

"We will be as quiet as possible…" but that was all Sinbad was able to say, because Ralf Gunarson charged past howling madly swinging his massive axe as if it were a toy.

"No you fool!" Sinbad shouted, but it was too late.

Ralf Gunarson attacked the wizard, seeking to separate the man's head from his shoulders.

But Ralf's howl of rage betrayed him. By now Abdul Bel-Fideel had Kaleel Al-Suarazi on his knees and by the throat. The black robed sorcerer turned at Ralf's roar and snapped his left arm behind him in Ralf's direction.

A bolt of jagged lightning sizzled and snapped from his outstretched fingers, impaling Ralf in the chest and hurling him back to the hard stonewall. He slid down its surface, unmoving.

"Ralf!" shouted Tishimi.

Immediately Henri pulled arrow after arrow from his quiver and loosed them upon the black wizard. But the sorcerer was even faster; his fingers spread wide and the arrows burst into flame the moment they left Henri's bow, arriving at Abdul Bel- Fideel's feet as ash.

But now Sinbad and Tishimi were both upon the evil wizard. The evil sorcerer tilted his head back madly, his grey beard raised high under his mad eyes. The black wizard unleashed a hellish assault upon them. Lightning streaked from his fingertips, but Tishimi's sword blocked it somehow. The magic lightning was drawn to her blade, as if it swallowed it all. Even Tishimi was wide eyed at this. But then her eyes narrowed and she began to advance.

Sinbad raised his scimitar and leaped to the attack, hurtling through the air, seeking to ram his sword through the evil wizard's chest.

But the wizard dropped the red cloaked sorcerer he had been holding by the throat, unleashing a blast of foul smelling wind that tossed Sinbad through the air, slamming him into the cavern wall next to the unmoving Ralf. "Fool! I am Abdul Bel-Fideel, and no mere sailor may end my life."

A cry suddenly tore through the room.

"Sinbad! Help!"

Sinbad turned groggily, fighting unconsciousness. But his eyes widened in shock when he finally focused on the person whose voice had called him.

It was Haroun, and he was leaping aside as the statue of the giant golden scorpion that had been above the altar now moved as if alive. Its monstrous tail jabbed again and again, killing sailors with one strike, impaling them and then hurling them away as if they were unworthy trash.

"Ooohhh." Moaned Ralf, next to Sinbad.

"Ralf, are you well?" Sinbad shook his large friend.

"Do you mean am I well enough to fight?" groaned the big Norseman, "Then the answer is yes. But I still feel as if the Midgard serpent had crawled up out of my guts."

"Forget your serpent, on your feet."

Sinbad forced himself to his own feet and charged back toward Tishimi who was parrying the mystic blasts of the black robed wizard repeatedly with her katana. But she could not advance on him.

"Foolish girl," the wizard sneered, "I am Abdul Bel-Fideel, and you are a child playing at being a warrior."

"I am no child, son of a pig. I am a samurai warrior." she cursed back at him.

The temple cavern was in complete chaos. Men were battling against the seemingly impervious giant golden scorpion, while Sinbad and the others were now arrayed against Abdul Bel-Fideel.

The sorcerer continued to vex them all with lightning strikes and blasts of wind.

"Enough wizard, you'll not win this day whilst I stand against you." Sinbad shouted.

"Foolish sailor, do you actually think to best one such as I?" the black robed wizard replied.

Now Bel-Fideel turned his attention to Sinbad. He raised both hands as if preparing an especially powerful spell, when the all but forgotten red wizard, Kaleel Al-Suarazi painfully wrapped his charred and blistered arms around his foe, holding him tight.

In Sinbad's sash the dagger called Grachene began to vibrate wildly. Without hesitation Sinbad gripped it and hurled it cleanly in one motion, impaling it in Abdul Bel-Fideel's throat.

The red wizard growled in his enemy's ear, "You may have killed me, evil one, but I will gladly drag you down to hell with me."

Instantly both men burst into a flaming pyre and turned to ash before Sinbad and his crew's astonished eyes. The accursed dagger Grachene dropped to the ground with a loud clank.

""Mon Dieu! What we have just seen! Things like that should never be witnessed by men who believe in God." Henri exclaimed.

"We must help the others," Sinbad ordered. He ran toward the giant scorpion, stooping low to pick up the dagger and place it back in his sash.

By now the men battling against the horrific gold scorpion were reduced to only five, Haroun and four others.

"This thing must die." grunted Ralf.

Henri nocked an arrow quickly and fired it into the joint on the foremost of legs. Instantly the scorpion fell over. "I got it!" he shouted excitedly.

But Ralf Gunarson was already charging past Henri, slamming his great war-axe against the scorpions golden hide. Again and again he brought his great blade to bear against it, each time denting its gleaming skin. Then finally with a roar Ralf sheared through the foreleg of the Scorpion sending it sailing across the room.

Before Ralf could even begin to enjoy his victory another leg lashed out and smacked Gunarson backward through the air. He landed in a heap, moaning loudly.

"This is madness." whined Haroun.

"No more so than other things we have seen like this, boy." Sinbad muttered.

"Aye you are right as always my Captain." the boy bravely replied.

Sinbad reached down to his sash once more, as if stung by something there. He glared at the crippled scorpion, which still fought to right itself while the men hacked at it ineffectively.

"Tishimi, you are with me, and pray to your father's spirit to aid you, for we now go to kill a god."

She nodded wordlessly and ran alongside Sinbad toward the towering horror before them all.

"Henri!" Sinbad shouted, "Its legs, cripple them. The rest of you attack the leg joints with your swords."

Henri stood back and released volley after volley of arrows blisteringly fast, each one finding its mark in the massive jointed legs of the creature. The crewmen followed with repeated stabbings and cuttings at the legs of the gilded monster.

Now the gargantuan scorpion was frenzied in its attacks slashing out repeatedly with tail and legs seeking to slay its attackers.

It opened its metallic mouth and released an ear splitting roar that forced everyone yet alive to cover their ears.

Sinbad turned to Tishimi and shouted "Now!" above the din. Both charged the mammoth creature as it reared up on its hind legs. Simultaneously Sinbad and Tishimi embedded their magic infused weapons into the golden creature's underside, tearing it along its length as they ran beneath it. Sinbad's dagger and Tishimi's katana tore through the gold skin as if it was paper.

With a thunderous cacophony the giant gold scorpion fell to the ground and split apart into simple pieces of forged gold, seemingly lifeless and unmoving.

Sinbad leapt to the altar where the princess Yasmine was still bound and gagged. He almost used the dagger still in his hand, but instead placed it back in his sash, where it abruptly vibrated once and faded from sight, its work done. Instead, he removed his trusty scimitar from the scabbard upon his hip and cut her bonds. Lifting the gag from her mouth, he carried her from the altar and placed her gently upon the floor.

"Princess…Princess," he urged, "Are you well? Can you hear me?"

Groggily her eyes opened and she saw Sinbad's handsome visage smiling at her.

"Oh, but who are you my handsome Prince?" Princess Yasmine whispered.

"I am a prince no more, beauteous one. Merely a sailor upon the seven seas. I am called Sinbad by most, the rest call me far worse." he grinned.

The girl in his arms looked at him and slowly smiled, her eyes matched the sparkling of Sinbad's own.

She then reached forward and kissed him upon the lips with much fire and passion, something they both enjoyed greatly.

Sometime later back aboard the Blue Nymph and already out at sea, "All is well my Captain?" Omar asked.

"Aye Omar as well as can be expected with a poorly repaired sail and half our crew lost."

Both men turned to a big grey cat that ran up to them carrying a dead rat in its mouth. It dropped the carcass at Omar's feet.

"Ah look my Captain; Samson has brought us a present."

Omar picked the dead rat up by its tail and flung it overboard.

"Now I must return the favor." Omar walked over to a net of freshly caught fish picked one up and quickly scaled it. Then he cut a piece off. Smiling he threw it at the cat, which swiftly picked it up and ran off, disappearing below decks.

Omar smiled. Samson the cat was one of the few things in life that made Omar smile. The occasion was rare indeed. He turned back to Sinbad, "So is all well with the Princess?"

Sinbad shrugged with a smile, "As well as can be expected, Omar. She is traumatized and needs much…attention."

"Aye my Captain, as I have surmised from your many trips to her cabin since we have left that accursed island."

"What can I say, Omar. We are all slaves to our own beauty." Sinbad smiled, then looked at Omar, and laughed, "Well, perhaps not all of us."

Omar turned away, frowned and began to harangue the crew while Sinbad walked to the bow of the ship, put his foot up upon the rail, looked out into the distance and smiled contentedly.

THE END

Why Did I Want To Write A Sinbad Story?

Well that's a fairly easy one to answer. I'm a huge sword and sorcery fan and what is Sinbad if not sword and sorcery? Plus, I have some knowledge of the character as I grew up watching the great Ray Harryhausen movies. When asked if I would be interested in writing a Sinbad story by Ron Fortier of the mighty Airship 27 productions I jumped at the chance.

But first I had to re-immerse myself in the character. I immediately added the three Harryhausen movies to my Netflix Queue, as well as ordered up the first Sinbad compilation from the Airship so I could find out what Airship 27's take on the hero was going to be.

After a few days of watching the Harryhausen flicks and reading the first anthology it was time to get cracking. I love writing action filled stories, and this was the perfect vehicle for one of those. Also, I have a history of writing Sword and Sorcery with my own 'Torahg the Warrior, Sword of Vengeance' novel which debuted last June from Pro Se Publications.

So with the story I wanted to tell in mind I set out to craft an ocean-spanning tale of Sinbad the Sailor and what you hold in your hands is the result. I hope you enjoy reading it as much as I enjoyed writing it.

RALPH L. ANGELO JR. - crafts tales from his secret enclave hidden in the middle of Long Island, NY a scant few miles from the shore. He has had a love of action/adventure novels and comic books since he was a youth growing up in suburban Long Island. Ralph has written epic fantasy, sword and sorcery, science fiction as well as New Pulp. All of Ralph's books can be found at http://RLAngeloJr.com. You'll also find information on his upcoming projects there as well. Ralph can be reached on twitter @ RLAngeloJr as well as on Facebook at https://www.facebook.com/Author-RLAngeloJr.

Ralph's novels include 'Redemption of the Sorcerer, The Crystalon Saga, Book One'. The Aforementioned 'Torahg the Warrior, Sword of Vengeance,' and his most popular creation, the sci-fi/space opera adventure, 'The Cagliostro Chronicles'. Ralph has two new novels awaiting their finishing touches right now. One is entitled 'My Enemy, Myself, The Crystalon Saga, Book Two' which is the sequel to Redemption of the Sorcerer. The second is 'The Cagliostro Chronicles 2: Conflagration' the sequel to the Cagliostro Chronicles.

Ralph is also an avid motorcyclist, skier and guitar player/singer.

Sinbad and the Isle of Madness

by Jeff "Venture" Fournier

"By Allah! Hemita, clear the docks for the last of it!" Omar bellowed at the slow moving longshoreman working to offload the Blue Nymph's latest cargo. The old seaman had to use his 'sea voice' in order to be heard over the din of the Yemeni port where the trade of copper, gold, frankincense and myrrh was thick and fast. Fortunes in the valuables of the overland and sea trade routes were exchanged here everyday. The bustle of the port and the wildness of the town attached to it was as if some mad frontier village had reached the sea and clamored for more space. Captain Sinbad El Ari and his crew stood armed and ready surveying the port. It paid to show that the fierce reputation of the Blue Nymph's crew was not idle boasting.

The bold captain of the Blue Nymph smiled at Omar's expression of the need for haste that the rest of his sailors felt. They wanted rid of the valuable cargo as well. The quicker the delivery the quicker they were paid and then the ship could pull away to a smaller less crowded cove he knew just down the coast. Not coincidentally this was located near a very dark and very wet fest hall that had the wine, women and song his men craved. Sinbad turned to survey his ship from his vantage point at the stern.

Sitting high atop the mast of the ship sat the Gaulish archer, Henri Delacrois. His cool glances around the port spoke of an easy casualness that was belied by his ready bow. Henri had a cloth yard shaft fitted to his English longbow and many in the port knew if the archer could see it, he could hit it. There would be no surprise rushing of the ship or her cargo by over eager traders today.

Standing unconcerned near the gangway to the docks was the Viking warrior Ralf Gunarson. He wore his immense broadsword and carried his ten pound ax at the ready watching the stevedores come and go on the ship as they shifted the immense bales of spices, some weighing a hundred pounds or more. There were grumbles among the sailors that Ralf could have lifted the bales himself off the boat two at a time. No one said anything to the Norseman however. The crew knew his skill with his weapons and his mighty temper was not to be roused lightly. Many of the curious passers by stared at the six foot seven giant as if he were a relic brought to their shores from some far distant land to be traded as a slave. One look in his cold blue eyes was enough to dismiss any connection between this barbarian from the distant north-lands and the word 'slave'.

Amidships on an empty water barrel rested Tishimi Osara. The lithe oriental woman sat contemplating the seeming nothingness of the ocean side of the ship. She wore her laminated Yori armor over black silk leggings and tunic which did not conceal her feminine curves from the rest of the world. The fact that she was unveiled and armed with a sword was seen as scandalous in some circles. If the ships passing on the seaward side could see her facial expression they would have thought her bored or perhaps drugged. Upon closer examination however they would note that she carried herself as a proud daughter of Nippon above such vulgar commerce. She and her samurai class ancestors had never engaged in the bustle of trade as the merchants did in her home nation. She would continue to watch the unprotected boat side until relieved or Sinbad told her to stop. The heat, thirst, or discomfort meant nothing to the young samurai engaged in her chosen trade. That trade was death, most accurately stopping it and dealing it.

"Captain Sinbad!"

Sinbad looked up at the source of the cry from high in the rigging. It was the youngest of the crew, Haroun. The sharp eyed rope monkey pointed far past the docks inland. "Many men wearing bright robes ride into the end of the Bazaar. They move with a purpose through the throng."

Henri bristled at having a young boy notice something before he did. "I see them. They appear to be monks of some sort. Who wears yellow robes here?" The hawk eyed Gaul sat straighter on the mast. He had a nose for trouble, and some of the best eyes among the crew.

Sinbad's handsome face scowled for a moment. "None I know of. Hindus? Perhaps they are looking for goods as well. Even monks need to buy food and spices." He moved to the dock side rail. "Are we done here Omar?"

The old sailor finished with the merchant who salaamed deeply and left with his cargo. "All done!" Omar tossed the small bag of gold up to Ralf who in turn threw it to Sinbad.

Sinbad weighed the pouch in his hand gravely. The crew would be paid with but only a little profit to show for the ship itself. The cargo that brought the greatest gold was gold itself. This spice trade was too slow for his tastes in earning coin. Another ship bringing something to port only a few hours before could cause other ships coming after to lose much profit.

As Omar moved to walk up the gangway to the ship he was stopped by a polite gesture from a weary looking traveler. He turned to eye the man.

"Are you taking passengers? I need a ship to the east," the man asked gravely.

Omar's reply died in his throat. The man was dressed in a full turban and a rich robe. Though travel stained and carrying a pack his eyes looked quick and intense in their gaze. He had the dust of many miles on his leather boots.

Omar bellowed. "Captain Sinbad! I have a man requesting passage on the ship going east." It was not uncommon for the Blue Nymph to have passengers but one man was hardly a cargo worthy of the ship's time. Sinbad made it a point to approve all who came aboard the Blue Nymph with few exceptions.

Moving to the rail Sinbad eyed the potential fare." We are sailing empty and my crew needs rest. Another time perhaps." He turned to go but was caught short at the sight of the man. He seemed familiar somehow.

"Allow me to introduce myself. I am Abdul, a poet and traveler from Damascus. I would very much like to leave this port immediately for any point near the Bengali coast." He was sweating and not because of the sun. Sinbad was wary. He had seen enough hunted men in his time. It was odd that a scholar would need to flee the city at his back.

"I would not lightly task the Emir by helping debtors flee the law. I must do business here in the future," Sinbad replied.

The poet freed a small pouch at his belt and opened it for Sinbad's inspection. "I have broken no laws of the Emir. Would a man with these need flee his debts good captain?" Inside the pouch was a wealth of pearls. "They are yours for my safe passage to Bengali."

Sinbad moved to the scholar's side and inspected the contents of the offered pouch. Inside was the wealth of a small caravan! To be sure some of the pearls were misshapen as raw pearls often are but there were many of a hue, color and size that he had never seen. Blue, black, green, purple, almost the entire spectrum of the rainbow seemed present in that scintillating pile. If real, their true worth and rarity could only be guessed at. Checking the color and feel of a green one Sinbad was surprised to find it genuine, not just some bit of paste with dye added to fool the gullible.

Sinbad closed the pouch and placed it in his belt sash. He waved Ralf aside and gestured Abdul to the gang plank. "Welcome aboard the Blue Nymph."

Sinbad gave a quick whistle and the young look-out was down the mast and on the deck via a shroud line. "Haroun will attend to your needs and see you to your cabin."

The young man helped the poet with his pack burden and then turned to Sinbad. "Those monks in yellow are making trouble in the bazaar and moving this way. They are starting fires and fights."

The poet looked slightly pale at his news but Sinbad calmed his passenger. "Go below. We will be leaving shortly."

As the man was lead away by Haroun, Sinbad gestured to Ralf and Tishimi who had moved amidships and joined Omar who had come aboard as the off loading had finished. "Raise the gangway and away all lines; we make for sea. Watch for trouble. There is a disturbance in the bazaar."

They broke and began moving towards the dockside of the ship. Omar signaled for the sail to be raised by the crew as Ralf and Tishimi dragged the gangway aboard. Other sailors began casting off mooring lines.

"What's this then?' the big Viking scowled as he tried to unlimber the plank.

"I am sure the Captain's reasons are sound," Tishimi replied as she bent to the work.

"Sound or not it will be slow going to leave the port. The wind is barely a breeze and we are too close to other ships for oars and poles." Ralf dragged the plank aboard by main force and quickly stowed it with a casual kick. "Henri! Come down and help us you lazy lout!" The archer had climbed half way up the mast to get a better look at their surroundings.

"Attend the docks! We are being watched," Tishimi hissed.

They turned and saw a most unusual sight. A full score of yellow clad monks watched the ship silently in a space that had cleared around them in the crowd. They wore full saffron colored turbans as the Bedouins did and carried various weapons and daggers openly. Both had seen monks in this land before but never armed or with such an air of menace around them.

The dock was only a few feet away but these men would have to be the greatest jumpers in the world to bridge the gap to land on a moving ship. Ralf ignored them, refusing to look away first. They searched the crowd with harsh stares and not a few lingered on the moving Blue Nymph. Several of them could be seen questioning others ships crews curtly about something.

One of the yellow clad men came forward and called to Sinbad. "Stop! The Satrap commands it! We would search your ship for a thief and a heretic."

Sinbad called back to them with an air of innocence, "We have no heretics here, just able seamen going on our way." For the life of him Sinbad could not remember hearing about a new Satrap operating near the port. He had never heard of a bandit leader that used monks as enforcers, ever.

Whatever the monk was about to say in return was lost as their new passenger chose this moment to peer out a window on the side of his cabin to see what was going on. Abdul's eyes set upon the Monks and he withdrew back into the ship and closed the window.

The Monks gave a weird cry and pointed at the ship. Quickly, several procured grapnels on lines and cast them up into the rigging of the Blue Nymph. Others shouted for their brethren.

"*Merde!*" cursed Henri from his high perch as a razor pointed grapnel almost took out his eye. He drew and fired on reflex. The shaft flew true and buried itself in the heart of the one holding the other end of the line. The yellow clad killer dropped immediately and all hell broke loose.

"Repel boarders!" Sinbad cried as he drew his sword and leaped to defend the aft deck. The ship was moving too slowly and having grapples in the rigging would impede making sail. "Omar! Clear those sails and set men to the sweeps!"

A half dozen of the yellow garbed, blood mad assailants began swinging over on to the deck of the Blue Nymph with murder in their eyes. They hit the rail or the ship side and leaped over. Others gathered on the docks with their weapons drawn, called by their remaining brothers.

Omar and two of the crew were in the rat lines trying to clear the monks' accursed grapnels from the sail as Ralf and Tishimi drove forward to meet the invaders amidship.

Three of the killers drew wicked looking daggers as they advanced on Ralf. The Norse warrior swept at them with his great ax leaving the sword on his belt for now. Its length made it too risky to the others in these tight quarters. A monk went down with a scream and a caved in ribcage as the ax bit deep and held. Experienced as he was in this sort of fighting Ralf knew that a simple tug on the haft with his foot on the body would free his weapon, only he never got the chance.

One of his opponents whipped a short length of weighted chain around the big man's ankle and gave a mighty yank, bringing Ralf to the deck with a thunderous crash. Like lighting, another monk was upon Ralf attempting to pour out his life with vicious dagger blows on the prone giant.

Tishimi Osara rushed forward to help her fallen comrade as other monks closed in around her from all sides. Each step she took was sure and precise as the cuts accompanying them. It was as if she were doing her usual 'advance and cut' exercises on the ship at night when the deck was empty. For each yard she went, another of the yellow robed fanatics was struck down. More tried to swing over from the docks trying to overwhelm her. A hideous whirl of steel and blood was woven around the young samurai girl and to bar her way across the deck was death.

She ended her walk with a final stroke that removed the head of Ralf's attacker in a lighting cut. Ralf kicked away the body as he freed his legs from the chain. Tishimi was breathing heavily after the blazing quick fighting movements.

"I can't believe you waded through them without being cut!" he exclaimed as he rose from the deck ready for battle. His own wounds so far were superficial.

Tishimi looked at him frankly and fell to one knee, resting on her father's sword with both hands clenching it tight. As she knelt, Ralf could see a veritable sheaf of knives sticking in her back armor like so many steel blades of grass. A small rivulet of blood dripped down one of her elbows to spatter upon the deck. "I didn't," she hissed through clenched teeth. Rising, she shook off the most shallowly embedded of the daggers as Ralf nodded to her and went aft. Tishimi nodded back and went forward. Soon they were engaging what few monks remained that were menacing the crew of the ship and trying to get below deck.

Sailors struggled on the deck in the general chaos of being menaced by the dagger wielding mad men as the crew tried to get oars out effectively. More of the yellow clad killers boarded nearby ships on the dock to leap from them on to the Blue Nymph as she passed. Soon the Blue Nymph would be out of the harbor and the ship would get away.

Omar had brained an antagonist with his own grapnel after freeing it from the sail. Far from being the grizzled Sindhi sailor near the later half of his career, Omar had fought pirates many times before. Seeing to the oarsman he smote about him with a knot of rope and a fist hardened by a life time of sea work to guard the crew as they worked the oarlocks. "Back you devils!" he bellowed as he dislocated the jaw of one attacker. "Pull for your lives!" he urged the oarsmen on.

Ralf's anger was terrible to behold as he waded into the monks. Ignoring clever sword play he lay about himself on all sides with broad sweeps of his blade. Steel crunched into bone as he lifted one foe completely off his feet with a shearing cut to send him back to the deck never to rise again. His pivoting back cut left another foe-man reeling with ghastly wounds he would only endure for the last few fleeting moments of his life.

Working towards the bow Tishimi came upon one of the saffron clad knife men as he set himself to dropping the ships anchor stone over the side as soon as he could cut loose its securing lanyards from the deck. With a sharp cry she buried her sword in his back stopping the chain of events that would have hindered the ships progress from port. As her sword lay tangled in the dying man another monk vaulted the rail and land only yards from her. His smile was a grim line around the knife he carried in his teeth. She quickly drew the deadly short blade she wore at her belt. Laying it over the warding forearm of her other hand she measured her attacker who secured his blade and gave a strangled fanatical cry. He reversed his knife and advanced to hook it quickly over her guard. Too late he realized his mistake as Tishimi's shorter blade was even faster than her longer one. A flurry of strikes and counter blows passed between the young girl and her attacker. In a flash of a distraction move he lost sight of her wakizashi for a split second right before it tore open his midsection. He fell to his knees even before he realized the stroke had landed. Retrieving both of her weapons the girl samurai went to seek more foes.

With a clash of steel Henri dropped his tangled sword. The two assassins he fought had tangled its guard with a combination of grabbing the hilt with a weighted chain and smothering his attack by dropping his point to the deck and stepping on it. Dodging over a barrel the Gaulish archer had no time to retrieve his bow from his back before they pressed him. Acting quickly he drew his dagger from his boot and struck the first attacker through his extended forearm causing him to drop his wavy bladed knife. Henri caught the falling dagger in mid air and rammed it into the man's heart. The second attacker tried to move to flank him but Henri towed the dying man on his knife around to block his approach.

The yellow turbaned killer grabbed his former cohort and threw him aside then struck with a lunge. At the last moment Henri twisted to the side, letting his opponent's knife pass by his body. Clamping his arm down to control the knife hand he pushed his own steel into the man's chest past his flailing guard. Dropping the corpse he regained his sword and made ready his bow. After a quick survey he scaled the mast with his bow in his teeth held by its string.

Sinbad parried the stroke of a whip wielding attacker as he maneuvered to defend the pilot's station at the stern of the ship. If the raiders took control of the steering the sluggish current here would drag them into another dock or ship instead of escape. The cut and thrust of his flashing sword worked against the cracking of the barbed whips the monks facing him used. He knew it was only a matter of time before they tangled his blade and disarmed him to face their daggers. In a split instant one of the two monks sprouted an arrow buried up to its fletching in the junction of his neck and shoulder.

Hanging upside down from a line above Henri Delacrois had made the shot from such a high angle to avoid hitting Sinbad. Momentarily the final zealot's attention flickered as Sinbad's blade thrust for his chest in a flash of steel. Sinbad completed his thrust with a quick riposte. The mortally wounded monk lashed out with a knife that came within a hairs breadth of spilling the captain's life on the deck. The yellow clad killer went down with a groan and died. Sinbad confirmed that the man was dead and looked around warily. Henri freed himself from the rope and climbed down to join his captain. He quickly crouched to the deck to retrieve the arrows that had dropped from his quiver during his acrobatics. The archer was breathing hard. "These men die hard captain, but it was a pretty shot!" he grinned.

Sinbad nodded grimly. "By Allah, they spend their lives like water! Go forward and help Ralf." Never had Sinbad faced men more willing to cast their lives aside for a chance at hurting their enemy. The terrible master of these fanatics must be dreadful indeed to inspire that kind of frenzy. He could see that Omar had cleared the grapples from the rigging while Ralf and Tishimi heaved dead cultists over the side. The fighting was over. None of the monks had been taken alive. A few of the crew were wounded but none badly. Dropped knives and bodies littered the deck like debris after a storm.

Far away onshore Sinbad could see the rest of the Satrap's devotees had gathered where the Blue Nymph had been docked. A palanquin had been brought forward through the throng of yellow clad fanatics. It made its way silently on the backs of mute slaves without hindrance as the crowds in the port had been run off by the whips and rage of the monks. As the bearers rested the shrouded platform on the ground its curtain parted and a overly tall man stepped out. He was clad head to toe in saffron colored robes with weird arabesques and designs. His face was completely covered by a thin wisp of yellow silk. The leader of the monks had an air of sinister purpose about him. From his far vantage point Sinbad could see he was a black man of some sort but most unusual. The parts of his skin that showed were the shade of dark slate. It must have been a trick of the widening distance from the port but he looked immense, lanky and almost seven feet tall.

"Omar!" Sinbad was ready to be quit of this place.

The mate was directing men aloft to quickly patch a small hole in the sail from a hook. "Aye Captain!"

"We make for open sea as soon as possible. Set course easterly for Chatgaon. May Allah grant we find a fair wind."

The mate returned to his tasks and mumbled quietly, "...may Allah grant we find nothing more."

Tishimi sat in Sinbad's cabin with her bare back exposed to Rafi as he worked on cleaning and treating her wounds. "It doesn't look like the blades were poisoned. Only a few even got through your armor." The old physician worked carefully and slowly, daubing medicine on the least of the wounds after cleaning them. "One or two here will need to be sewn up. Should I get Omar and his sail needles?" he joked.

Tishimi Osara smiled slightly and shook her head at the physicians attempt at humor. "No! Have you seen his sewing?!" The small laughter had made her wince at her wounds a bit.

Sinbad knocked on the cabin door before entering and closing it behind him. He always tried to be respectful of Tishimi's right to privacy aboard ship but was relieved that she was fully robed while Rafi attended her. "How bad is it Rafi?"

"Mostly minor like the others. There are a few deep ones but they will mend in time. She should take rest for a few days at least to give them time to heal." The thin old man who attended to the crews hurts replied. He heated a needle over a lamp and prepared a length of cat gut.

"Tishimi you will stay below for a few days resting" Sinbad ordered. "Our guest will sleep in the spare cabin."

He saw her start to protest at sharing the below deck areas with a stranger. "I would know he is watched by one I trust." the captain concluded. The female samurai nodded as Rafi set to work.

Sinbad returned to the deck. Omar had the ship on course and Haroun was on look out. The weather was pleasant and a good wind was blowing in their direction of travel. They were making good time. Yemen was leagues behind them now. He noticed Haroun's gaze lingering to the stern as if looking for pursuit.

"The horizon is clear Captain Sinbad!" he called as he noticed the captain watching him. Sinbad waved in acknowledgment but even his own gaze wandered over their wake. He could see nothing but he could not shake the sense of being pursued.

The Greek ship cut through the waters at great speed even in the deepening twilight. To sail at such speed at night was very dangerous, even with all lanterns burning. Striking a hidden shoal or reef at speed could destroy a boat, killing all aboard. No man on this ship feared death by drowning anymore. The yellow pennants snapped in the wind as the craft slid through the waters searching for its prey.

From deep on board could be heard the muffled rites of the obscene cult of the Saffron Satrap and his followers. A frenzied cacophony of bestial cries culminated in a broken shout and silence. Later a bloody parcel was cast overboard as the mate went to the pilothouse. "Full sail on this course until the sun dawns," he growled to the helmsman. "The apostate will not escape us...not escape *him*." The pilot nodded and held course on the blinking red star the Greeks call Aldebaran.

Sinbad was relived on watch by Omar and went below for the evening meal. He found an unexpected sight at the table. Their passenger was entertaining them with a tale of the frozen north from Ralf Gunarson's homeland. The Viking sat with a look of rapt attention on his face as the storyteller regaled those at the table with a heroic fight of a northern king against a monster and his mother. When the tale was ended the men gave their applause, none more enthusiastically than Ralf who pounded his mug against the table in the applause for the yarn.

"Captain! Come sit! Abdul here knows the most wonderful sagas." The north man spoke with a child like excitement in his voice. "I have not heard that tale since I was a lad. Where did you hear it storyteller?"

Abdul bowed modestly in recognition of the compliment then took his seat. "I first heard it from a noble in Baghdad who traveled extensively amongst your kin good sir. I was his guest for some time"

Sinbad started, "That is where I know you from Master Abdul! It was many years ago but I recalled your face and manner. You are Abdul Al-..."

"Speak it not!" The Arab interjected. "That name used to be a source of great pride for my family, now it is a constant threat of danger. I have taken a new name to protect any of my family that remain from my folly. You may call me Abdul Al-Hazred, I have used this name many times of late to pass among strange men in strange lands."

Sinbad frowned slightly at the alias as he sat down to eat. Strictly speaking it made no grammatical sense in Arabic and could be interpreted many

"Abdul, here, knows the most wonderful sagas."

ways. One would be 'Servant of the Prohibited', a mildly heretical title at best. Another interpretation that made less sense was 'Servant of the Fenced In.' Both ideas troubled him.

"Are you in the habit of passing among dangerous men? Your pursuers seemed to know you on sight." Sinbad continued, "Should I be looking for yellow robes in your bags Al-Hazred?" His hands rested casually on the dagger hilt in his sash out of view under the table.

The poet looked very long in the face and shook his head negatively "I was never formally admitted to the Order of the Saffron Satrap. He did not, strictly speaking, know I was talking to his devotees. There was much they sought to learn from me about…strange matters. I was hoping to learn more of their ways but alas I provoked their notice and then their ire after asking too many questions."

"Their ways seem rather dangerous." Tishimi spoke evenly from her spot at the table. Even now she sat leaning forward so as not to put pressure on her wounds.

"You have no idea young woman. They are the right arm of an evil power that lurks hushed and unseen in the dark places of the world. They move in shadowy ways and with grim purpose. Their actions in the market today were much bolder than the usual way they deal with their enemies. Many are the times I have walked the halls of deserted cities and sought the knowledge of unsavory things so that I may defend myself from them."

"You stole the pearls from them?" Sinbad asked bluntly. His trust was not so easily given.

"Nay, good captain I acquired the pearls many years ago on an Island when I was completing one of my studies in astronomy. The oysters they came from lay scattered on the beach in heaps as if piled like some child's toys left unattended."

The eating at the table stopped. Ralf and Henri's eyes flashed at Sinbad who asked the obvious question. "What was the name of this island?"

Al-Hazred paused reluctantly. "I called it the Isle of the Lotus. I do not believe it has any other name. It is in the middle of the very sea we travel on. When it is there at all."

"It is a disappearing island? This is a fable Sinbad!" grunted Ralf as he lifted his tankard to wet his suddenly dry mouth.

"There are many cycles in the universe," Al-Hazred began. "When the tides move, when the moon wanes. Not all of these are known by man. Is it so hard to think that an island has a time 'it is' and a time it 'is not'? I have studied the stars for many years and have gained some insight into their movements in relation to these cycles. In a month's time or so the Isle of the Lotus will be for a day and a night and then it will 'be not' again."

Sinbad rose and gathered charts from a cubby hole on the shelf. He unrolled one and laid it flat on the table in front of the mystic. "Show me."

The scholar looked at the charts and seemed reluctant to speak further. "I would not treat my host's request with disfavor, but I would warn you to have a care. There are things man was not meant to see and places where his tread should never have fallen."

"We have dared places like that before and lived to tell the tale," Sinbad smiled jauntily.

"I know. I have heard those tales." The poet thought a moment. "Still, I never did finish my observations there. It would be good to complete the task if possible. I will show you the spot and consult the stars tonight if the sky is clear." The adventurer and the mad Arab bent to the table and consulted the map.

"He's mad!" Henri hissed to Omar, Tishimi and Ralf who had gathered on deck in the moonlight.

"There is no treasure that sits upon a sandy beach for men to simply take."

"Sinbad believes him," countered Ralf, as he drank in the salty night air. "I would have thought a treasure that you could stoop down and put in your pocket would have great appeal to you."

Bristling at the jab slightly Henri let it pass. "I do not like cults that hail from the waste places of the world. I have seen this before."

"Where?" The Norseman stopped in mid stride.

The Gaul looked thoughtful and when his eyes again met the Viking's they were tinged with a long forgotten fear. "When I fled my home those many years ago I was pursued through the mountains and valleys for several days by the Lord Mayor and his men. I managed to shake them off and rested for several nights in the stone ruins of an abbey in the mountains. On the second night I thought they had found me but it turned out that it was just a band of men who had traveled to the abbey on some errand. I hid outside and watched to see what they would do." Henri visibly blanched and his already pale features were white in the moonlight, his voice scarcely above a whisper.

"I will not speak of what I saw and heard." He shuddered, "It was enough to burn them all as heretics had any witnessed their atrocities. I crept away and ran all night as fast as I could. By dusk the next day I came upon a port and bought passage on the first ship to the east." Henri looked relieved as he unburdened himself of his tale, his jaunty attitude returning. "I will someday return to my homeland a rich man but I will never do so by way of that vale in the mountains."

"Bah! There will always be mad men aplenty in the world, but how often have you stepped on new lands before all other men? It will be good to see this place and take its riches if they be there." Ralf smiled. The Viking way was as ever his guide in life.

Tishimi spoke, "The Arab will be paying us a pouch of pearls whether we find this Island or not. The ways of many poets and scholars seems strange to most. I believe this man is a bit touched but no malice flows from him. If we can make a fortune off this trip, why not?"

The three nodded silently as they watched Al-Hazred on the bow gazing at the stars and making notations in a book he carried.

Aboard the Satrap's stolen ship there hung an air of waiting. The mate and the rest of the crew were on the deck, all eyes looking for sign of the ship with the blue sails. A sign was promised them today by their inhuman master. If the augury of the previous night was successful they would know what direction the ship with the apostate sailed.

Suddenly, the Satrap was there among them. All bowed to his fearful presence and prostrated themselves on the deck as he walked forward to the side of the rail. He touched a part of the worn wooden rail and chuckled slightly. Using his talon like fingernail he dug out a curly ribbon of teak wood as if using a carpenter's gouge. He held the curl of wood for a moment and then brought it under his face cloth as if to whisper to it. When he brought it forth from the wrappings it was no longer a bit of wood but a Toredo worm that writhed and flopped in his palm. He cast into the sea and it floated on the surface for a moment, then began to swim away from the ship in a direct course.

The Saffron Satrap pointed in the southeasterly direction the worm was going and his command was clear. The sails were hoisted and the ship began to follow the wake of the worm. Strangely the creature's wake grew larger and larger even though the worm was at quite a distance. Soon the worm had left the ship behind but her crew had sighted in a course following along to catch the prey it hunted...if there would be anything left after the worm arrived.

After many days at sea the Blue Nymph was making considerably less time. It had tacked into the wind to stay on its southeasterly course since leaving port. For several days now though they were becalmed and at the mercy of the current. This combined with short rations had made the crew grumble a bit but Sinbad kept his men busy repairing the sails, cleaning and general ship's work. Ralf and Henri gambled with dice on their off watch hours and Tishimi found herself growing to like the company of Al-Hazred. He had a quick mind and was fascinated by what poetry and tales she could remember from her homeland. It had been so long since she had interacted with someone of a cultured bearing that she almost felt awkward.

Many of the strange Arab's hours were spent bent over a large bound book of notes he worked on in his cabin. Rarely did he take the air outside unless it was at night to take readings on the course and the movements of the stars. This bothered most not at all as the crew had begun to think him a bit touched anyway.

Sinbad noticed Omar acting strangely this morning as the watch changed. The sea was hazy and the wind only now starting to pick up. The grizzled Sindhi mate stood at the mast and was leaning on it with one hand as if to comfort himself with its solid presence.

Sinbad knew trouble in the offing when he saw it. "What is it Omar, breakfast not sitting well?"

Omar looked up with grim seriousness. "I have not eaten yet. The sea... the sea is wrong somehow." Many decades of life on a ship had given Omar a sense of all the sea's moods. He knew her as a man knew his wife.

Sinbad took his unease seriously and scanned the waters around the ship and the sky as such could be seen through the breaking fog. He spied no ships, no danger, no errant waves. Surely the old salt was just having an ill met morning.

"The sea smells wrong," Omar stated bluntly.

Sinbad did not notice anything at first. Then it crept upon his senses as gradual as the dawn. There was no smell of hidden land. No salty spray that belied bad weather or the wet plant smell of kelp covered reef. Then Sinbad caught it and his nostrils flared.

Blood. The seas smelled of blood.

Omar spoke plainly. "We are entering dangerous waters, Captain."

"You worry over much old friend. We are not even at the island yet. The Sea has its moods."

"Aye Captain." Omar moved off to attend to ships duties as Sinbad went to the taffrail to check the course.

Suddenly the ship shuddered as if scrapping over land. The crew lurched on deck and looked over the side. Nothing could be seen in the water but an up swell of current.

"Have we hit something, a reef?" Ralf asked as he rushed to the deck.

"I took a sounding not a moment ago, there was at least twenty fathoms beneath the keel," Omar cried moving to look over the side.

Sinbad dropped a scrap of canvas over the side rail. It passed lazily behind the ship. "We are still moving, but very slowly. Perhaps we are caught on an old fisherman's net? Omar send a man over the side to check the hull."

Kev, the best swimmer of the crew stripped to his breechcloth and cinched himself in a loop of line so he could be lowered over the side. Sinbad gave him a ship's knife. "No heroics. Look and come back up and we will decide how to proceed." The young Moorish sailor nodded.

Haul up the slack!" Omar called as he and Ralf made the line taught as Kev climbed lightly over the rail. He hit with a splash, bobbed a moment, and then went under. Almost immediately a pair of sharp tugs pulled the line from below signaling he wanted to be brought up. They hauled him quickly out of the water and to the deck. He sat shaking as a man plunged in cold water, not as one who left the warm sea. He grasped Sindbad's arm in a death grip. Words tumbled from his lips in a insane chatter. "A worm! A giant worm is chewing upon the ship! Allah protect us, it is huge!"

The Blue Nymph lurched again and the crew all felt a shudder. They knew now it was the monster gouging into the hull with its jaws of hard bone designed to bore into wood. Had the Blue Nymph's hull been like other craft of her day she would already be going to the bottom with all hands aboard. Only her metal fastened teak wood hull had saved them this long.

Omar scurried to the hatch even as Sinbad shouted, "Omar! Check below for damage! Ralf, a grapnel and line long as a ship length. Hurry!"

"Haroun! Pass out axes to the crew. All hands on deck!"

Sinbad joined Ralf at the bow where the Viking was using a rough whetstone to make sure the tines of the grappling hook he held were as sharp as possible. "What are we using for bait?" the big Viking joked grimly.

Sinbad did not appreciate his humor when the ship was in danger. "We are the bait. Halve the line and rig the hook in the middle. We will toss the hook over the front and drag the line under the boat from both sides. We will hook it, drag it up and cut it to pieces."

Ralf finished tying a figure of eight on the bight to secure the grapnel to the line as Sinbad separated the crew into two groups, one along each rail from bow to stern.

Ralf tossed the grapnel over the bow and the crew began to tow it to stern along the bottom of the boat. Abruptly it caught on something amidships and the lines in hand jumped like a living thing. The whole vessel gave a heave out of the water slightly and Sinbad knew the hook was set. "Put it through the block! Heave it aboard!" Sinbad cried as his crew struggled to manage the lines. He rushed to stand upon the topmost deck to see what they brought up. The crew pulled as one on the other end of the line.

Presently with a great heave they reeled in the monster over the taffrail. The hook had snagged the beast mid length and was buried deep. The creature had the shape of a elongated worm, what some of the sailors knew as a Toredo or boring worm, grown to hideously fantastic proportions. It was fifty feet long and as big around as a hogshead barrel. Its slimy, pale flesh undulated disturbingly as it thrashed trying to get free. The hard armored plates of chitin dug gouges into the deck as it tried to find purchase to move itself off the deck and back into the water. It made an inarticulate grinding noise that sent shivers down the spine.

Ralf leap to the monster's head and crashed an ax blow across what passed for its skull. The steel clashed dully upon the worm's armor plates but did not bite. Other members of the crew hacked at its fleshy sides opening great rents that gushed yellow ichor.

Henri readied his bow for a shot. The creatures thrashing made the deck slick with slime and debris as it slashed around in search of prey to grind with its mandible plates. Pulling a shaft almost to his ear he let fly at what he hoped was a vulnerable spot. The broad head arrow sunk into the flesh with a meaty thunk out of sight leaving only the nock at the end protruding. Enraged the creature turned its way trying blindly to crush whatever had hurt it. Its thrashing knocked several of the crew off their feet and even grinding one to pulp underneath its horrendous bulk.

Tishimi chose that moment to strike with a devastating cut to the monsters back. Yellow and green ichor burst everywhere and the stench of rotting wood permeated the deck. Her Katana left burnt blackened edges on the monster's wounds, proof that its supernatural origin could not protect it from the enchanted power of her father's blade. It reared up its head and body to slam down upon the young samurai with a force that could splinter a ships hull. Hurling herself sideways the samurai put the mast between the beast and herself as she struck a great rent in its side.

With a flash of a tigers leap suddenly Sinbad was there! He had swung from the top deck upon the monster's back in a fit of rage. Holding on as if he was riding the worm like a pony he sank his dagger into the flesh behind the head for purchase and hacked the neck of the worm with a flurry of sword thrusts. Ralf had never seen the captain so near a berserk state in battle. It would seem nothing would draw it out of him except a physical attack upon the ship he loved.

The creature went mad and reared up trying to shake off its attacker. "At him you dogs!" roared Ralf. The crew ringed the monster striking with axes feebly at its immense bulk. Tishimi and the big Viking dove in to open the wound from her previous slice to encompass the whole of the monsters width. Finally with a great double handed blow from his ax Ralf separated the creature's body in two. The rest of the crew used boat hooks and deck pikes to drive the flopping tail half of the wounded monster to the edge of the deck and soon the ocean beyond.

The rest of the creature made no noise. Its only sound was the sick squelch of blades in its flesh and the grind of its chitin plates on the deck. As it rolled its death rattle Sinbad leaped clear, shouting "Watch out for the head!"

The monster's great chitin beak clacked futilely, slowly ceasing as whatever weird life drained from its body. By now the crew had a good hold of the line still hooked in the monster. Using pulleys and throwing the line back and forth over its bulk they held it pinned to the deck as it death throes abated. As soon as it was truly dead they heaved the body with tackle over the side. The deck was awash in strange slime and smelled like a rotting pine forest.

Sinbad looked over the carnage as the last of the monster's flesh was washed over the side by Omar and the crew. Loose barrels, bits of plank and ropes were scattered around in a mix with blood from the creature and at least one of the crew, crushed by its bulk during the fight. Thankfully there was no damage to the mast.

The waiting waves heaved the monster's dead carcass up as if the ocean itself spurned taking such an abomination into its depths. Sinbad cleaned his dagger and sword on a bit of scrap cloth. As he went to the side and tossed it in the sea he noticed Omar staring perplexed at the worm's remains. Already there were sharks circling the corpse of the beast. Blood would draw them for miles he knew.

"By Allah! Look, Sinbad. Those terrors won't even eat of its flesh!" The grizzled sailor was correct. Not even the man-eaters of the ocean seemed to want to partake of the worm's carcass. They swam in circles around the ship for a few minutes, bumped the corpse a few times with their snouts then glided away as quickly as they had come.

Regaining his poise the captain clapped him on the shoulder. "Would you?" he jested.

Omar smiled slightly but did not seem as light of heart when he moved away to check the hold for damage the worm might have caused below the waterline.

Several days after they encounter with the sea worm Sinbad and Al-Hazrad both agreed they were very near the spot the scholar thought the island would appear at. This was good, as the ship was becalmed. No wind stirred the sails and the ocean was a placid lake of green glass.

"Omar! Run out the sweeps. We will row for a bit." said Sinbad.

The first mate grunted and called for the oars to be put out as the crew bent their backs to it. "What course captain?" cried Henri from the pilot station.

"A point off east." Truly Sinbad did not care what course they took. Even several hours of rowing would not take them far. It was more important for the crew to be doing something than worrying about an island they could not see yet. Plus they had many periods of inactivity punctuated by the occasional desperate moment in the last few weeks. The activity would do them good.

With measured beats they drove the great ship forward under Omar's cadence. Tishimi and Al-Hazrad looked over the side at the calm water. Its surface was stirred only by the dip and pull of the crew's oar strokes.

"It is unusual to see someone from the Far East, especially a person such as yourself. I have never met a Samurai so far from home." The poet had been fishing for Tishimi's story for some time on the voyage.

The Samurai girl looked distant and tried to act humbly. "I am never far from home on the deck of the Blue Nymph. What of you? I met many poets in my land but none who lived with danger at their heels. How came you to this?" said Tishimi.

Al-Hazrad's eyes grew dark and his brow furrowed in consternation. "You yourself are a smith of fine words young warrior and yet you are here? Have not the writings you've shown me over these last few weeks illustrated that danger and loss can temper some artists as a piece of iron in a fire?"

Tishimi looked with mixed emotions at the scholar. "Sometimes you are forced by events to go and do things that were not how you planned your life. It is the way of the Samurai to accept what comes and move forward. My writings are but an echo of the past I once had, receding as I go into the future."

Al-Hazred nodded and continued. "Such is always the way. I used to be a courtly spinner of tales and a learned man of note. Now I am a wanderer searching for knowledge that only I know is there. It may be the death of me if I continue but it will certainly be the death of me if I stop. Certainly that is not death..."

The scholar's words died in his throat as he noticed Tishimi's staring downwards into the ocean's depths. Past her gaze he could see forms under the clear water.

They were sunken ships. Hundreds of them strewn here and there relatively intact and covered with sea growth. The Blue Nymph glided above them serene and untouched as if floating above a vast graveyard like an angel on an errand.

Suddenly a wispy shape darted from one undersea wreck to another. Very soon they could see others moving about in slow processions. Even from here high above she could see they had a feminine form, grotesquely wreathed in weed and wrack. Tishimi looked to Al-Hazred.

"They are some form of wandering spirits." the poet offered. "In the high deserts where in the Djinn and Efreet dwell I have seen these she-devils. They are the eaters of the dead called 'ghoulehs' by the tribes. They are very dangerous. We must make no sound to draw their ire!" The Arab began praying at a whisper but no devout follower of the Prophet would have recognized the words.

"All quiet on deck!" Tishimi hissed at Omar who whistled quickly and made the gestures for silence on deck to the crew who repeated it to each other until everyone got the message. Sinbad joined them at the rail. "What is it?"

Al-Hazred gripped his arm. "They are the female spirits of those who killed themselves in grief over lost sailors. They search for their lost men. We must not rouse them from their wandering below. They would be most violent."

At that moment Terali the cook came from below with the slops from the ship's kitchen. He noticed everyone standing silently and saw one of the other sailors give the sign for 'no talking'. He nodded and went back

...a wispy shape darted from one...wreck to another.

to work, quietly dumping the scrap bucket over the side as was normal for ridding the ship of waste. He saw no reason to be concerned.

As the slop hit the water with a meaty slap those of the crew who stood looking over the side gave a gasp. Below the fell creatures twitched and looked above. With a powerful stroke they shot upwards and out of the water to land on the deck. They landed with a wet noise as the water ran off their bodies to pool upon the planks. "To arms!" Sinbad cried as he squared off against one of the she devils that stood before him. She was a hideous sight.

Her body was naked, deathly pale and slick with the slime of the sea. Her hair draped like sea wrack and her face was both beautiful and terrible to behold. The eyes were black and carried an ocean of torment in them. Her mouth was a razor trap filled with teeth like an eel's. She staggered forward as quick as a crashing wave. Sinbad struck with a quick thrust and cursed as only black water gushed from the wound. The monster screamed and clawed at his head with a raking grasp. He twisted free getting nicked on his cheek and swung a fully committed back cut in return. He lopped its head off even as it grasped him and tumbled to the deck. With a curse he broke free of the dead embrace and rolled to rise and get back into the fight.

A dozen more of the monsters had landed on deck as well and a few had already dragged several other screaming crew overboard in their cold clammy embrace to be drowned below in the monsters' lairs.

Henri stood amidships and managed to loose an arrow at one of the attackers. The shaft made a wet sound and passed completely through the Ghouleh's breast and tore through its black heart and out its back. The creature did not seem affected and it leaped on him in a crippling embrace that was cold and wet. Henri fended the monster's snapping jaws from his throat with his bow. He could barely keep it off until he could get a boot under it and vault it over the side with a splash. He slung his bow and drew his short sword to strike one of the monsters that was tearing at the throat of one of the crewmen like a jackal.

Tishimi was menaced by two of the gaunt figures which she promptly beheaded with a sweeping cut. Her father's sword was proof against super-natural creatures and the edges of the lethal wounds she dealt were black and smoking as if charred in a forge fire. Her weapon seemed to be the most effective one they had against the monsters' rubbery flesh. As the two fiends fell she pushed past them and began striking their cohorts. Very soon the shrieks of the maimed and dying monsters became the dominant sound on the bloody chaotic deck.

Ralf was grappled on all sides by a half dozen of the fiends "Off me you devil bitch!" he roared as he caved one's skull in with his ax. Another of the creatures grasped his arm and sank its teeth into the chain armor protecting his bicep. It grated the links between its jaws like a reef stroking a ships hull and blood began to well from the wound. With a shout to Odin the Norseman cleared the deck around him with a slash of his sword. Having gained a moment's respite, he bodily dragged the creature still holding on over to the mast and bashed its head against it with such force that the rigging shook. After the third such blow the Ghouleh released his arm and he could do a proper job of pulping its brains out against the stout wood with his bare hands. He dropped the now lifeless carcass to the deck and gave it a savage kick for good measure. Rising with the blood mad fury of the berserk he took up his sword and hewed into another one that sprang at him.

Cowering by the wheel with Omar, Al-Hazred grasped a torch in passing from a flaming brazier and used the fire to fend off the growling and snapping she-devil coming up the stairs. He knew charms to keep such monsters of the high desert away but they would take too long and might not work against the Ghouleh. He started to say them over and over under his breath as he waved the sputtering torch back and forth. With its flame out from the vigorous motion and idea struck him. He used the charred tip of the wood he held to inscribe a symbol in the deck with the charcoal.

Creating a poem at the spur of the moment he cried, "O friend and companion of night, thou widows of the ocean mire, who wander in the midst of the sea among the wrecks, be gone!"

It was not his best work but the intent and the symbol was clear. With a lamented cry the fiends backed away from the barrier he had erected. It seemed to be working.

Sinbad was slashing left and right. The monsters seemed able to take hideous wounds and still keep coming long after a living being would lie shrieking in pain on the deck. They grasped at his shirt tearing it in their cold talons as they attempted to drag him to the ocean's embrace. Whirling, he suddenly realized he was trapped against the rail by three of them. The center one of the trio spoke with a chilling, distant voice. "You are a captain! A captain for us, sisters! He will sail us around the ocean depths to find our lost men." Her eyes watered as she grinned with glee.

"Why not?" Sinbad gasped. "Have you a ship below that is seaworthy?" He was stalling for time. As he spoke his eyes darted to a line that secured some of the barrels the ship carried stowed upon the deck.

The cruel mavens of the deep saw his gaze and realized what he was about. They moved well away from where a rolling barrel loosed by a cut rope might crush them as it broke free.

Right into the trap he was really springing. Sinbad pulled a knot loose from the main mast sheet that held the yard arm still on its tack. The sail's yards long timber swung in a wide arc. He had timed it perfectly with the roll and pitch of the ship. It crashed into them with hammer like force, pulping them over the deck with a sick crunch. He quickly made after the loose line and secured it fast so as not to endanger any of the crew.

The rest of the monsters had slunk back to the sea and did not seem inclined to pursue the matter. The few injured crewmen were already being tended to by Rafi. They were lucky but should not tempt fate.

"We seem to be on the edge of their territory. Who feels like a night of rowing?" Sinbad called.

A crowd of hands rose as one.

The morning after the incident with the Ghoulehs had started bright enough. Then the sky had turned angry with a chill wind howling through the formerly slack sails. Ordering the canvas brought down Sinbad looked to the horizon to the south to see if any trace of the storm front could be seen. The clouds boiled with titanic lighting illuminating the sea for miles around. The ocean churned as if stirred by Poseidon's trident itself. Never had Sinbad looked upon such a quickly changed sea. "Rig for storm! Close the hatches! Ralf take us into the wind!"

Al-Hazred and come on deck and struggled to the captain's side as the deck began to heave in the ocean like a living thing. "It is the island, Captain! We are near and it will be soon!" The poet had a glazed look about his eyes in the light of the raging lightning storm. Sinbad ordered him below. The deck was no place for a landsman with a storm brewing.

"Tsunami!" Tishimi cried as she pointed to a spot a few points off the bow. The frothing crest of a wave miles off began to stretch itself along the front half of the horizon. The wall of water was moving fast towards them and towered above the ship even at this distance.

"All crew set to lines!" Omar made each man fast to a safety rope around their waist. It might save them from being tossed overboard in rough seas but the crew detested wearing the things as they hampered them when they worked. Ralf and Henri staggered back to the helm as rain and spray coated the deck. Henri was not as sure footed as Ralf on the slick deck and the big Viking had to steady him as they made for the tiller. They both made themselves fast to the rail with hastily tied rope.

"When it is about to hit we will have one chance." Sinbad explained as he joined them. "We must come hard over to port and ride the face of the wave to the crest. Once we are over this one we will be back in the trough and gain speed for the next wave to do the same. If we are lucky we will face lessening waves as we go."

"And if we are not so lucky all those times?" Henri croaked as he shook off the spray of water that doused him.

Sinbad's reply was drowned out by a crash of water over the side as the ship spun on its new heading into the wave front. The bobbing ship was tossed about the ocean roughly as he maneuvered it into position to ride the first wave. There was no more time for talk.

The tidal wave came at them like an avalanche of water as high as the ship's mast. The last friendly rays of the sun were bent to a jade green in the depths of that titanic surge. The Blue Nymph skidded along the face her blue sails snapping in the wind. With a mighty heave of the rudder Sinbad turned her course up and into the wave front. The force of the tons of water heaving past the keel and rudder was like a thunder-stroke shock to Sinbad's hands on the tiller. As the ship made way up and along the face of the giant wave he almost lost his grip on the rudder, then Ralf was there. He braced himself on the opposite side of Sinbad taking up the strain of the opposing forces of wind and water on the ships rudder. He watched for cues from Sinbad to lessen or increase his iron grip on the ships steering. His arms shook with the strain and his face turned ruddy as his iron thews locked the ship on the course Sinbad chose. There would be no second approach, no return from that wave front if the Sindhi Captain did not time his turn perfectly.

The Blue Nymph shot like a skittering stone up the front of the wave. When it seemed beyond all endurance that Ralf and Sinbad could hold the course any further, they were over it in a slow instant of momentary triumph. Then the ship rode down the back of the wave like a boulder picking up speed down a mountain side.

"All hands brace!" Sinbad cried, the roar of rushing water tearing away his words almost as he spoke them. Even Ralf who was standing next to him did not hear as the bow of the ship dug into the swell at the bottom and heaved up at a steep angle. The front of the ship drove under the green sea for a moment up to almost amidships threatening to capsize the vessel as Sinbad harshly threw the wheel with Ralf's help on to a sharper course change to get them ready for the riding of the next wave.

The Blue Nymph's namesake prow figure, a mermaid affixed to see the ship's way safely, exploded out of the water and rose up with its gathered momentum. She pointed ever forward, with a smile on her wooden lips, as she sped up the front of the next lesser wave behind the one they had just passed. The water gave her breasts and tail a polished sheen that made the figure look almost alive, bobbing in that ocean of raging water. The next wave was more easily handled, and the one after that. Hours later the Blue Nymph and her crew were settling into the ocean at twilight once more, drenched and battered but alive.

Omar tallied the crew and all were accounted for except two men. The frayed ends of snapped lines on the rail bore mute evidence of their watery death at the hands of the merciless ocean.

Ralf lay in silent agony as his overtaxed muscles locked up in rigid protest to the efforts they had been called on to give. Sinbad hung on the wheel as he too tried to regain his strength. Henri moved to spell him as the captain moved across the ship checking lines, mast and crew as he went.

"I like not the look of the hull, captain. We will need to careen her and check for damage from the worm and the wave," Omar spoke as he returned from checking below decks at the foot of water in her hold. The practice of 'careening', tipping the ship on its side to inspect or repair the hull, was not an uncommon one and Sinbad himself had done it many times.

In a calm sea, at a good port.

"We will see to the ship as soon as we find the island. Let me know if it gets any worse."

Al-Hazrad was gasping for air as he emptied the contents of his stomach over the side. "Surely the plagues of a thousand devils hound my stomach." Tishimi watched over the ill poet in the darkness as Haroun and a few others began to try and relight the brazier of damp coals that had gone out on deck. Everyone was soaked and the task looked impossible.

Sinbad remarked to the poet, "I am not sure how far off our course the wave has taken us. We will have a better bearing in the morning as it is too cloudy to read the skies tonight."

"Nay Captain, the wave proves that we are close. When it rose so violently it must have rent the ocean asunder as it came into being. Set a watch to the east and we may sight the island by the morning."

"Botros! Take first watch at the helm." Sinbad ordered.

"Aye Captain!" The sailor nodded and went to his station. The rest of the crew cleaned the detritus from the storm off the deck and set about drying what they could by hanging clothes and articles from the lines.

Later that night the scream of a madman roused the crew who were off watch. Sinbad bare chested and grim with his sword drawn met Ralf halfway up the gangway to the deck. "What the devil?! Is that Botros?" Henri joined them as he strung his only recently dried bow.

The three stood in the unusually chill night air as they scanned the deck with only the barely flickering brazier as light. Botros was not at the tiller on watch and Ralf quickly rushed to take control of the ship. A quick survey from bow to stern was made to find the errant sailor. The rigging was empty as was the lookout perch.

"He is here!' Tishimi called. She had risen silently from her bed at the first shout and had made her way up through the forward hatch. She stood on deck with her naked blade gleaming in the moonlight. She was barefoot and had wrapped herself in a hastily donned cloak tied off at the shoulder to give her freedom of movement. She would have gone into battle as she had risen, stark naked, but she had grabbed the cloak to better conceal herself in the darkness.

Sinbad blanched at her near nudity. He was no prude, but the first time Tishimi had defended the ship when awoken at night by Malay pirates it had almost caused the Sindhi crew to mutiny over the effrontery. Thankfully she had put something on, but Sinbad knew from experience that she would fight in little more than a sheen of sweat and the blood of her foes if the occasion called for it. Their culture and her warrior code sometimes made for bewildering combinations.

She stood near the forward rope locker in a ready posture that gradually lowered as she examined the scene. Botros was there sitting amidst the lines. He was tying bowline knots in the ropes over and over again. He occasionally gave a shout or a gurgled laughter as he completed a knot, then he began another and another. Dozens lay about him on the deck. The light of sanity had gone out of his eyes and he drooled wordlessly in madness as he tied the same knot over and over. He murmured an old sailor's rhyme that was used to teach how to tie the knot.

The hair on the back of Tishimi's neck rose in hackles. "He is ill Captain. Not of his mind. Possessed?"

Sinbad looked on in grim horror. He was baffled by what could do this to a man. Botros was a sober sailor and not one for flights of fancy. Something he had seen on the watch had turned the young sailor into a drooling lunatic. He saw the crew starting to mutter among themselves on deck. Best to keep them busy.

"Bind him and take him below to his hammock. Omar, see that he is cared for by Rafi. Clear the deck!" Sinbad ordered. The crew jumped to as ordered. Sinbad turned and walked aft with the young samurai at his side.

Omar, with a look of pity on his face, took charge of the broken sailor. He tossed the lines Botros had knotted over the side. He knew no sailor aboard would undo those bights. Botros went as if he was a small child being led to bed.

Henri approached with a lantern all aglow. "We are checking the ship for intruders. So far we have found nothing." Whatever had taken the sailors sanity had never even been on board the ship.

Sinbad called to Ralf at the helm. "Take the watch till dawn, I will then relieve you." He knew that Ralf feared nothing. If the Norse man saw a soul shriveling horror he would ask it how the fishing was.

The bare-chested Viking nodded and kept his attention on the wheel and the sea ahead. "It is chill this night. Tishimi, I could use that cloak." He grinned.

Without missing a step the samurai girl whipped the cloak from her shoulders and furled it up to be taken by the wind to Ralf. She had timed it just right so that as she left its shelter she entered the dark shadows of the gangway passage down to her quarters. There was barely a flash of skin or a hint of steel as her nakedness was enveloped by the velvet darkness below deck. She had practiced moving about the ship at night so many times she no longer needed a guiding light to find her way.

The fluttering cloak caught Ralf full in the face. He pulled it off with a deep rolling laugh and tossed it unneeded to the side. He had endured far colder climes than this night and the opportunities to jest with the Japanese warrior were few and far between.

Sinbad wished he could as easily toss off the pall of events as he went back to his quarters to try and sleep.

In the morning, the day had dawned clear and bright. Within miles an island was sighted. The beach was unnaturally white sand and the craggy rocks were covered in lush plant growth that towered to waves of hills upon which the riotous growth had spread. The Blue Nymph circled the island once to find the best place to put in. A large rock outcropping on the northern side stretched like a natural quay many yards into the ocean surf. As they moved closer Omar's soundings found no reefs, only sand and broken basalt blocks of weirdly unnatural regularity in shape. It was if the island was thrust upwards from the ocean depths on a pedestal.

The air about the island was filled with the heady perfume of tropical plants. The sickly sweetness of the floral scents was punctuated by hints of incense smells and cassia. Overriding it all was an eerie sense of quiet. No birds flew, no fish played near the ship. It was as if the island was unfurnished somehow.

"How do the jungle growth and plants lay so dense on what was only a few hours ago under the waves?" Sinbad asked Al-Hazrad.

Al-Hazrad shook his head slightly. "I know not. It simply is. The riotous growth you see today was as I saw it those many years ago when I first set eyes upon the island. As I'm sure it has been since the beginning of happenings and will be until the end of days."

Sinbad gathered the crew around the mad poet. "Al-Hazred has been here before. Listen well to his warnings."

The Yemeni scholar looked suddenly self conscious then warmed to talking on the subject.

"The chief danger on the island we found was the flowers it is named after. Every kind of lotus known under heaven grows here in great quantities always blooming. The very air is permeated with their perfume. Have a care, some of the lotus blossoms are of rare varieties, Black, Red, or Blue for example that have certain narcotic properties. One great whiff will send a man into a deep sleep haunted by dreams of vivid reality. Others will make him a slave to any whim voiced to him; still others will bring death or madness at a single breath."

Haroun covered his mouth and nose. "We can all smell them now! How are we not dead or mad?"

Sinbad cuffed him on the back of his head for such foolishness. Haroun moved his hands away from his face quickly to his sides.

"It seems that the air of so many varieties of the dangerous lotuses growing together will confuse their properties over a wide area leading to no ill effects. We noticed no such maladies on my last visit," Al-Hazred replied.

"No wandering off the beach when we land," Sinbad cautioned everyone. They had found a swath of white sandy beaches only a half mile or so from the rock quay the ship was sheltering by.

"The oysters bearing the pearls you seek are on the sandy beach clinging to rocks that are now out of the tide. It should be a simple matter to collect them and find the pearls, good captain," the Arab finished.

Sinbad clapped his hands to signify the meeting was over and urge the crew to action.

"Omar you are in charge of the ship when we land. I need five men to go ashore with Ralf, Tishimi, Henri and myself. Have them bring many baskets. Then take the ship over to careen it and begin repairs. We must be ready to leave before the island sinks back under the waves tomorrow morning"

"I would like to accompany the shore party captain, so I may finish my observations of the island." Al-Hazred begged.

Sinbad nodded his assent. He would only be underfoot on board during the repairs. He turned to his warriors as the crew dispersed to their duties. "I want you all heavily armed. The rest of the men will be burdened taking loads of oysters and pearls to the ship."

"Do you expect trouble?" Henri asked as he tightened up his sword belt while loosening his sword in its sheath.

"Allah does not create an island with wealth unguarded strewn about the beach," Sinbad mused as he adjusted his sword in his sash.

"I for one look forward to the feel of an unknown land under my boots," Ralf smiled. The renown of Viking explorers was well known as nigh insatiable and Ralf was no exception.

Tishimi was looking on the island. She was already fully armed and armored. "It reminds me of some of the islands of my home." She turned and went to the weapons rack in her quarters and selected a long Naginata as well. Home held bad memories.

Soon the small landing party was on the shore. The white sands looked as if waves had just washed them perfectly clean. The footsteps of the crew were the only mark upon them as they made their way along. There were a few large boulders and groupings of basalt rocks and they indeed seemed to have a wealth of many crustaceans growing upon them. No life stirred on the beach as they walked it.

Henri moved forward and used his belt knife to pry an oyster free. With a few deft strokes he opened the strange looking shellfish. With quivering fingers he poked around inside until with an exclamation of surprise he pulled forth a small round green pearl. All the eyes of the men lit up and soon another and another shell was broken open as the crew dispersed to the task. Practically every one yielded a pearl of various shades like the ones Sinbad had seen before.

In an average day of pearl fishing three boatloads of oysters would be needed to find as many pearls as they had picked up in so many minutes. The men looked at each other as if in a dream. Sinbad grinned. "To work you fishermen! Gather as many shells as you can here. Sadir, Kev, begin

...he pulled forth a small...green pearl.

opening them and place the pearls in here!" He snatched Ralf's spiked helm with a quick motion and stuck it in the ground. Ralf laughed as he saw the wealth being poured in the impromptu bucket.

The men fell to with a will and very shortly a great number of the weird opened shellfish littered the beach. Every one yielded a pearl of varying hue many like normal pearls, but each greater than the one before. Occasionally a cry would rise as a particularly fantastic specimen came to light. Sinbad found a golden hued one the size of his thumbnail. Ralf pulled a sky blue one that he swore bore the luster of clouds in it.

"*Watasumi no me!*" Tishimi cried out in Japanese as she let fall the shellfish as she saw the pearl it produced. "Eyes of the sea goddess, look!" She held up the pearl for the crew to inspect. It was the size of a quail's egg and completely clear as glass. Within it was a tiny octopus that had been caught inside as the pearl formed around it. It was perfectly preserved for all eternity in a priceless prison.

Sinbad felt a cold shiver of unease at the sight. Henri peered at the rarity. "I have never seen or heard of a clear pearl. It must be worth a ...." he stammered at a loss for words, then looked around warily. "What place is this?"

Abdul looked amazed, his eyes alight with wonder. "That is what I came here to find out!" he quickly strode down the beach stopping to make notes in his book.

Sinbad gestured to Ralf and Tishimi, "See that he does not wander off." he loosened his own sword in his belt and began guarding the working sailors on the beach himself.

The Viking and the Samurai went after the scholar as the crew set to with the captain gathering up the wealth of an unknown land.

Aboard the Satrap's ship the crew shivered from the cold and wet of the previous night's waves and rough seas. The Satrap had predicted the weather well in advance and they had managed to keep the ship afloat and on course. On course to where only he knew. The Satrap sat in his cabin perfumed by heady incense and less definable odors. Now and then they shivered from a mixture of ecstasy and fear.

The Satrap sat in quiet contemplation. The signs and portends he had extracted from the universe had lead him to realize the apostate and his ship had made for the Island of the Lotus. He knew of course that was not its name. It had an older name with darker meaning and it had nothing to do with flowers. The heretic had sealed his doom by fleeing to such a place. The Satrap reached for the box before him on the altar.

It was of old teak and inlaid with symbols that twisted the eye. Opening it revealed that it contained a small wooden figurine of a squat frog like thing. It was crouched low like a toad and carried what looked like an ivory tooth in its misshapen mouth as a dog would carry a bone. He removed the tooth from its mouth and picked up the toad in his other hand. Where it touched his dark palm a red stain was evident. Taking the tooth he raked it over the back of the toad thing along a series of spines that ran down the figure's back. A warbling croaking tone sounded and vibrated off the hull of the ship. He repeated it at intervals and soon all the crew could hear the sound carry over the waves and water until it was like a living thing set loose upon an unsuspecting universe.

Initially Ralf and Tishimi thought the exploration of the island was only supposed to be a cursory one. Its hills were covered in riotous jungle growth. Palms, ferns and other less identifiable flora covered much of these. The trees were tall and seemed to be of various types never seen by either of the well traveled warriors. There were indeed many flowering plants, all lotuses as Al-Hazred had described. Blues, black and red and green abounded and the explorers gave them a wide berth as the poet expounded on what he knew of a few of the varieties.

"This Black one brings deep slumber like unto death. Look here! It is the rare Purple lotus rumored to have been used by the sages of Mnar to perfume their sacrificial altars to propitiate the dread Dweller Between the Sands. This is amazing! All the varieties I have heard of and many I have not seem to be here in profusion! Perhaps this is where they all came from?" He scribbled in his book as he paused for a moment. Here and there he gathered specimens to press between the pages of his journal.

Ralf knelt on one knee and checked the sandy soil for tracks. The deadly flowers held no interest for him "This ground is fairly dry considering it was under the waves yesterday. How are these trees here? Did they spring up as soon as the sun hit them?"

Tishimi shrugged her shoulders in answer as they followed Al-Hazred deeper into the jungle. The scholar was peering all about but what he hoped to find was a mystery. Presently they were out of sight of the beach and under the shade of the jungle trees.

After a half mile or so of hacking through the undergrowth they came upon a small stream of water, barely a creek, running across their path east to west. It was as clear as crystal and nothing stirred within its banks. There were no fish, or insects or other common inhabitants of such a tributary. Ralf dipped his hand in and tasted the waters lightly with his lips and spat. 'Brackish! We will not easily find water in this place."

They both looked up as Al-Hazred gave a cry. "By the Old Ones! There is something here!" the poet was staring at something up ahead and when Ralf and Tishimi joined him they could see he had found a clearing of sorts. It was not unoccupied.

A massive stone structure rested here at an odd angle. It was as if the building had the mud and plants form around it. The structure was unlike any the three had seen before. It stood at least a ship's mast high and was dominated by a portal shaped like an oval on its side. It appeared to be a massive door with no handle or hinge. Crooked blocks of black basalt led up to it and away to disappear into the ground amid plant growth at the base of the structure.

The whole pile was covered in vines and lotus flowers. Beneath the plants were weathered relief carvings. They varied in quality and subject matter. Many depicted strange glyphs and grinning toothy faces. Some showed scores of octopuses crawling up a hill bearing a terrific burden which had been long ago worn away by time and tide. The effect of the whole structure was one of brooding lonesomeness crushed into the mud by the weight of time. Strewn about were some smaller blocks that might have been the bases of other structures or remnants of columns of stone that had fallen over to rest on the ground over time. None were smaller than thirty feet long and Ralf struggled mightily thinking of how they could have been moved into place on this terrain. All were thicker than he was tall and had the weathered look of bedrock exposed to the wind. Each must weigh as much or more as the Blue Nymph herself.

Al-Hazred stood agape with his hands limp. He muttered things under his breath as he studied the structure. His visage held the look of one who had found the piece of a puzzle long sought, but in doing so had uncovered more places to fit others at the same time. He quickly put reed pen to ink and began scratching in his notebook hastily. The scholar had found a treasure trove of knowledge.

Ralf turned to Tishimi who was examining the base of what must have been a statue but its subject had long ago withered away. She knelt with her sword in her one hand as she brushed the muck of ages from the plinth of the statue, her spear stuck erect in the mire besides her.

"What is it?" he asked as he approached. She jerked with a start. She had not heard his approach or realized she had drawn her sword as she examined the stelae she had uncovered. The young samurai's face was plagued by conflicting emotions.

"I have seen something like this before in a book when I was home. It was a gift to me from Batu Kamito the night he announced he would marry me against my father's wishes. He thought to frighten me before he took me as his bride. It was the night my father died." She grew grim. "I knew he was evil, but to think he had sunk to the depths of the things these carvings showed."

With a curse she kicked dirt on the scene revealed as she recovered her spear and stalked away. Ralf saw only a glimpse of the picture obscured. Some scene with a woman being despoiled by a group of octopuses. He spat upon it as well and added his own curse as he defaced it with the hilt of his ax. The gods and monsters of other races held no fear for him.

"Have a care barbarian!" cried Al-Hazred as the sound of metal on rock broke his reverie. The scholar looked around warily. "Some things that lay undisturbed for eons can be awoken by the foolhardy."

"Let them come!" Ralf gestured with his ax. "We have gone too far afield already. We must return to the beach and the treasure."

Tishimi lightly touched Ralf's arm. "There is something in the trees to the north." His gaze swept the entire tree line but could detect no movement. Ralf moved forward and stopped at a toppled stone obelisk to crouch in its cover. He saw nothing in the trees that could have alerted Tishimi's senses. With a start he noticed fresher carvings for the first time on the rock in front of him. Tishimi and Al-Hazred joined him as he stared. "These are the runes of my folk." the big Viking said, a little disappointed to find proof that he was not the first Norseman to tread these shores. He studied the carvings crudely chipped in the stones edge. The same runes were inscribed over and over again.

"What do they mean?" Al-Hazred asked.

Ralf spoke. "It says '*Kjøre*' over and over." The Viking drew his sword and hefted his ax at the ready. "It means 'run.'"

Dragging the protesting sage with one hand Tishimi and Ralf moved back along their path through the forest. As they disappeared under the canopy a shadowy thing crept from tree limb to tree limb and silently followed them.

Ralf moved like a jungle cat, senses alert for an ambush. Suddenly a shape swung from a low hanging branch and dropped to the ground. Barring their way it reared up. It was the strangest sight any of them had ever seen. It moved upon legs that were tentacle like, supporting a long tapering body with no head. Its arms flailed about its environs as it felt around for prey or to get a better footing. The creature had a smell of wet rocks and rotten oysters. Its face was devoid of nose with only a pair of protruding globes for eyes. It looked like a large octopus and lay there blocking the path back the way they had come from.

The weird being looked at them with milky dead eyes and its only sound was a gasping shuddered breath as it inhaled air and drew itself up to a height of almost six feet. It stood on its legs as if they were stilts. It gave a hissing raspy cry like a drowning man searching for air. Suddenly another of its kind dropped from the trees around the trio and rushed to the attack. Al-Hazred was leaped upon and grappled to the ground with one around his backpack, its cruel beak hidden on its underside tearing into the object looking for flesh.

Tishimi ran it through with her sword careful to not accidentally stab the scholar. With a silent leap another had a crushing grip around her mid-section from behind. Its powerful arms clung to the laminate armor as its beak worried her armored back with a steady clacking and cracking noise.

"Bastard!" Ralf grabbed it with both hands and attempted to pull it off with a grunted effort. Its skin was dry but its body structure made it difficult to gain a grip. "Get it off!" the samurai yelled as the dead one slipped off her sword. Ralf was bodily lifting both the creature and Tishimi off the ground. The monsters grip was so strong it would not yield and Tishimi stumbled and fell into the nearby stream as the monster started to apply such crushing force that her armor flexed and her ribs ached painfully.

They both disappeared beneath the surface as Ralf grappled with another of the beasts that had dropped from above and tangled his arms. He roared as he swung the thing with both hands into a tree trunk. The tentacles seemed to slack and Ralf realized the beast was dead as it slipped off his hands leaving only red circular welts where it had made purchase on his arms. Al-Hazred sat in the stream with a small knife drawn as a pitiful attempt at a defense but none of the monsters came near him. Ralf backed up as more of the tentacled horrors dropped from the trees on the riverbank to gather and flail at them. Some stood on their legs as if on stilts and swayed along the river's edge. Some supported themselves hanging from low branches. They made only the hissing breathing noise and did not advance.

With a gasp Tishimi rose from the water the pieces of her dead attacker still clinging to her armor.

"Thor's goats! That was a close thing. Can you walk?" Ralf hissed

Tishimi nodded. "It seemed to die as it touched the water, even before I cut into it. I have never heard of an octopus moving out of water so well. How are they breathing on land?" She righted herself and helped Al-Hazred get up. The scholar sent a splash of water at the strange monster in anger and noted how they fled from it momentarily.

"Curse it how! Let's leave before they follow us." Ralf had his weapons out and was ready to fight but not here. Even now the dozen creatures at the water's edge were making their way back up into the trees to move around the water obstacle they apparently feared to cross. Al-Hazred gathered up his spilled notes and joined the other two as they moved through the jungle back towards the distant beach.

On the other side of the stream the tentacled abominations rolled and twisted in silent fury at the sight of their prey escaping. Soon they were joined by dozens more of their brethren and they began to fan out the length of the river bank looking for a way to cross the deadly liquid barrier.

With a few hours the men had made three trips to the longboat for more baskets to hold the pearls. Sinbad and Henri grew restless on the beach guarding the men. Soon they were spread so far that the captain and the bowman were forced far apart from each other watching over their respective beach ends.

Henri noticed noise amongst the rocks. A tapping sound as if rocks were being knocked together. Creeping forward with arrow ready he came upon a bizarre sight; a pair of octopuses were in the space between two rocks working to open a bivalve of enormous proportions. The shell was easily a foot and a half across. With a crack the creatures broke open the mollusk, discarded the fist sized red pearl inside, and began feasting on its flesh. They had been using a stone as a mallet to break it open.

Henri blanched at the ferocity of the creatures as they tore it apart. He moved to be away when one noticed him with its round liquid eyes. With a start, the bowman took as step back as the creatures reared themselves up on their arms to almost the height of a man. They darted towards him with a shambling gate as they raised rocks to bash at him.

Henri was astonished for a moment and recovered his senses in time to jump back off the rocks and put some distance between him and the unnatural sea life. He turned to sprint up the beach and warn the sailor who was gathering pearls nearest to him. The man was down on the sand stretched lifeless as a octopus similar to the others began to entangle his head with its tentacles and body. Henri raised and let fly an arrow at it and as it connected he heard the sickening crunch as the man's skull gave way to the crushing grip of the monster. His arrow hit true through the creatures eyes and he saw its arms release and curl about itself in its death throes. The sailor's head was a pulped mass like a broken eggshell.

"Sinbad!" he cried as he turned and put two quick shafts into the beasts coming out of the rocks behind him.

The captain turned with a start. From the other end of the beach he could see the Frenchman loosing a shaft at a stilted looking thing that lunged from the rocks. Suddenly there were a dozen around him and the other sailors gathering pearls. Two were dragging one of the crew between them by his feet to the cover of the jungle to be devoured and the other octopuses moved quickly over the sand to menace the rest of the men upon the stretch of beach. The crewman fought back with knives or spears or whatever they had at hand. The creatures grappled arms and legs and put their crushing beaks to hideous use on the bodies of the fallen. Sinbad rushed up and drove a pinning thrust downward with his sword to kill one of the monsters as the men fled back to the rock quay where the boat was moored. "Don't let them cut us off from the boat!"

Grabbing a standing spear left nearby Sinbad took aim and cast it at one of the monsters. The spear flew true and bowled the monster over as another rushed forward. To the Sindhi captain's surprise the other creature grabbed the spear with its tentacles and pulled it free to use on another passing sailor. Suddenly Henri was at his side loosing arrows at the monsters on the beach advancing towards them. Sinbad made it to the quay in time to be in a pitched melee with one of the monsters. The creature used three swords it had taken from the dead as adroitly as any swordsman he ever faced. He parried its triple cuts as he constantly avoided another tentacle trying to grasp his foot. The unblinking eyes of the creature never wavered as it attempted to get between him and the sea. Thinking quickly he kicked sand into the creatures eyes followed by a lighting fast sword thrust.

Just then Ralf, Tishimi and Al-Hazred broke out of the jungle with several of the octopoids in pursuit.

"To the boats!" Sindbad yelled to one of the sailors struggling with a basket of pearls. "We have a boat load already. As soon as the rest are here we shove off." The sailor nodded and began to ready the oars with another crewman to put as much distance between them and the island as they could.

Rushing at them from and unexpected quarter Ralf lead the way breaking through the line of hideous creatures. His sword bit deep, splitting one of the creatures as he used his ax to cleave another in passing. Al-Hazred dodged around the twitching corpses left in the Viking,s wake and made for the rocky quay that lead to the ship. Tishimi vaulted over one of the creatures as its swing with a rock went wide. She turned and cut it down leaving it to die writhing in the surf.

The big Viking gestured to the Arab to get in the boat as he took up a defensive line across the stone pier with Sinbad and Henri.

"They are all through the trees Sinbad. They swing on them like apes. To walk on that island for more than a few hours is a death sentence." Henri let loose his last arrow and made for the boat. The jungle canopy was churning as the creatures rushed forward from cover the beach in a tentacled mass of terror.

Sinbad nodded "We make for the Blue Nymph. Everyone aboard?" The Frenchman and the samurai nodded as they surveyed the hundred or so creatures that writhed angrily on the beach at the waters edge. "Look!" Tishimi pointed with her sword. "They will not touch the water."

The young samurai was right. The monsters stayed at the edge of the surf and scuttled back as any wave broke close. Presently they were underway and out of range of even the few small rocks the tentacled horde could throw at them.

Al-Hazred looked over the beach full of monsters. "Look! They eat the oysters, but will not leave land! I must make notes." He fumbled about in the ruin of his backpack and produced a battered but still functional tome and began to make notes with a charcoal stick.

Sinbad was enraged. He grabbed the Arab by the nape. "Did you know these things were here and not think to tell us?" His bloodied sword in his hand drew Al-Hazred's attention away from his scholarly pursuits.

"Nay my good captain. When last I was here we never left the beach and saw no trace of them. I swear by the powers I had no idea the isle was so dangerous."

Sinbad let the man slip from his grasp. He could tell the mystic held fear in his eyes but no deception. Sinbad grabbed the tiller and guided the boat to the nearby cove where the Blue Nymph was tipped slightly on it side and repairs were underway.

Sinbad jumped carefully aboard and checked the angle of the deck before moving. The whole ship was listing to the side over the water almost ten degrees off true. On the approach they noticed men working in the water on the exposed side of the hull to patch damage caused by the attack of the worm. Haroun sat on the rail overlooking them with sword and bow ready in case they should be attacked while working in the water.

Omar helped the sailors aboard with their basket burdens of hard won pearls. "The ship will be ready in a few hours. The repairs will hold until we get to a port and can make them permanent." He noticed Sinbad was coming aboard with less crew than he left with and the grim wounds on the survivors told of the battle's horrible toll. "We sail at dawn, Omar! Get these damn baskets of pearls stowed below and send Al-Hazred to my cabin!" Sinbad barked as he strode across the deck.

Later in his cabin Sinbad regarded the scholar over a cup of Ralf's stout mead to cool his temper. "I must apologize for my outburst on the boat before. I do not like to lose men, no matter what rumors you might have heard in the dens of sailors. What is it that drives you too such dangerous studies? I have never met a sage who seeks out such harrowing adventures."

The life and vitality seemed to drain from the Arab's face as he toyed with his own cup. "Once you begin pulling at the string of the mysterious fabric of the universe with learned inquiry you will see some of its glory shining through. The paths I have trod however have torn great swaths away to show me the yawning black abyss behind life and time." The adept's mood seemed to fall inwards as he sipped from his cup.

"Why do you keep tugging at them?' Sinbad replied.

Al-Hazred looked up with a shudder and a touch of madness in his eyes. "There must be some light there somewhere..."

In the morning the crew awoke well rested. Rafi had tended to what wounds he could and by dawn's early light the crew began to row around the island at Sinbad's direction. They would need to circle halfway around to be on course for Bengal and the wind had not yet risen. The weather was very fickle in these waters. The crew settled into the comforting sounds of a ship at sea underway which helped to dispel the horrors they had witnessed on the island. As the Blue Nymph cleared land a ship appeared on the horizon. Haroun called down from his view in the tops. "Ship Ahoy to port bow! Many men aboard and she flies only a yellow pennant!"

"The ship is Greek," Sinbad muttered as he eyed her moving to intercept the Blue Nymph, "but I know not its captain or name." Sinbad was not worried as the stranger's ship was being handled badly. Its sails were up and slack with no wind even as its oars dipped clumsily in the water. Its double bank of seventeen oars spoke of a sizable crew. Even with only its oars the Blue Nymph would easily be able to cut inside her turn and avoid her. Whoever crewed and commanded it were no seamen by trade.

Omar called for quiet, "Listen! There is a strange noise coming over the waves."

Omar was right. The crew heard it now as the others came on deck. It was a clicking noise. It came over the water on sharp regular intervals and seemed to echo from the direction of the strange ship. Its origin and purpose was unknowable.

Al-Hazred staggered up from below deck and ran to the rail to gaze upon the ship with terror filled eyes. "He has found me! The Saffron Satrap has come seeking vengeance on my head!" He stared in abject terror at the closing vessel.

Sinbad grabbed the fearful scholar. "The same one from the docks? By Allah he should have hired better sailors then! Be at peace Abdul, we will outdistance him by nightfall." Turning into the radius of the big ship would be easy for a vessel the Blue Nymph's size. The others ships bulk would be its undoing.

"Nay Captain! He is not of this earth and will hunt me to the end of days for what I have seen and learned." The Scholar moved to the side rail and sat on a coil of rope as a man awaiting an executioner.

Sinbad gave a call. "Omar, turn to sharp to port in twenty oar strokes and then lay on the speed. We will pass the island by and leave him little room to turn and pursue us."

Omar acknowledged and went about his tasks. Al-Hazred lifted his eyes to Sinbad's. "I fear catching us by ship is not his game. The Satrap's cult is devoted to many dark gods and he knows uncanny ways in which to influence them."

Sinbad and the crew jerked up with surprise. A spectacular booming crash filled the air as if a large stone had been tumbled to its side. The noise came from the island interior and echoed even over the waves and deck noise. The crew stood stock still. The clicking noise from the Satrap's ship had stopped and a low guttural chanting, as yet indistinct in its nature, carried over the waves.

The skies began to turn an ugly slate color. The wind and waves became more erratic and choppy. The wind was in their favor. Sinbad awoke from the momentary shock. "Ship the oars and raise sail!"

He glanced to the port side and stood dumbfounded. The island was settling deeper into the ocean. Already the surf had covered the beach and was beginning to rise over the trees on the shore. The land mass was returning to the sea from whence it came.

The crew broke the momentary spell of dread and set to the task. Omar exhorted them to greater speed as Ralf, Tishimi and Henri joined Sinbad at the wheel. "Henri, fire up some pitch and feather their sails as we cross the Satrap's course." The Frenchman nodded and stoked up a brazier nearby, setting a cast iron pot of the stuff therein. The pine resin was useful in repairs but burned devilishly when a coated arrow was set aflame and sent into an enemy ship.

"Ralf, you and Tishimi take two men each to a side. Prepare to repel boarders. Axes and swords will teach these scum that we are not prey to be chased." Ralf nodded and grabbed his ax. Tishimi drew her sword with a slight gasp. The blade glowed a pale blue fire. The four of them had seen the sword glow such when battling a supernatural foe, but never when an enemy was not present. It was as if the very air held a charge of eldritch menace.

Sinbad attempted to ignore the portent. "Get them ready!" He moved to the wheel and took over from Omar. The old sailor grunted as he loosened his own sword in its sheath. It had galled him to have fled the port being chased by these pirates. Revenge was a powerful motivator.

As the Satrap's vessel drew closer the crew aboard her gathered at the rails in a fanatical frenzy. They were closer now and Sinbad could hear there chanting cries. They yelled one word over and over "Sthaggua! Sthaggua! *Sthaggua!*" They all wore the same yellow robes as the cultists who had accosted them in Yemen.

Then they ceased shouting as the Blue Nymph passed by. Henri's first flaming missile arced over and touched off a blaze on their mainsail. He readied another then looked aghast. The crew on the cult's ship stood motionless weapons ready looking past the Blue Nymph doing nothing. They stood still as fire, the bane of sailors for ages the world over, began to chew at their rigging with licks of flame. They stood there with their leader, motionless, locked in a death grip of unholy fanaticism.

Henri looked at Sinbad who was just as bewildered, then he saw something out of the corner of his eye. "Beware to Port!" He cried. Beyond the Blue Nymph, between them and the rapidly sinking island, something great and terrible moved through the water. It created a swell like a great whale was passing and then madness burst from the sea to land on the deck of Sinbad's ship.

Born by a mighty leap the dread god the Satrap had awoken landed on the Blue Nymph and gave out a universe shaking bellow. Mighty Sthaggua was awake once more and hungry to destroy what had disturbed his eternal sleep. The thing stood almost half as tall as the mast. It was vaguely toad shaped with a thick fur like an ox covering its bloated body. Its four legs ended in heavy clawed paws as big as a barrel head. The fiend's half closed tri-lobed eyes burned the red of blood in the water. With an echoing croak it snaked out a tongue and snatched one the sailors standing near Tishimi off the deck and into its mouth with terrible finality.

Sinbad looked about for a pike to engage it at a distance but as the monster waded into battle with his crew he doubted if even the few yards of wood and steel would be much of an edge. Tishimi went forward and planted a horrible cut across its leg followed by an upward slash to its thigh.

The wounds her flaring sword left were deep and dark red ichor flowed from them as they began to close and heal at a supernatural rate. The monster snorted and stove in a yard of deck planks as it swiped at the dodging samurai as an elephant would an insect. Tishimi put the mast between her and the monster to gain a moment to devise a stratagem. The bestial god brushed against the mast and the whole ship shuddered at its touch.

Forming a quick skirmish line Ralf, Sinbad and the deck crew armed with pikes fought to push the monster back. Again and again they stabbed at it to little effect. Sinbad had gone to a locker on deck and brought out small shields for the crew. He tossed them to eager hands. With the new defenses the horrid tongue of the monster only lashed at the brandished shields unable to grab their holder firmly. The last time a sacrifice to the god had fought back humanity had not even developed shields so they confounded him mightily.

The thing was wary now, even though only Tishimi's blade had appreciably hurt it, the foul being suspected the others weapons might well be capable of that as well. It scooped up the longboat on deck and dashed it down at the crew splintering it asunder and scattering the men. It was so slow moving that they had managed to avoid it but the creature struck with unearthly power.

Henri sent his flaming pitch arrow into the beast's neck and was gratified to hear a gurgling hiss come out of the monster's frog like lips, but still it battled on. Ralf leaped at the monsters back, burying his ax in its bulk amidst its tangled fur. The edged turned, hardly hurting the beast. It slammed a paw into Ralf and sent him flying to the deck in a mass of pain ten feet away. Sthaggua paused to pull the arrow out of its throat and gaze

...it...snatched one of the sailors...

angrily at the still smoldering shaft as it renewed its flailing at the crew. The wound at its neck still bleed freely. Ralf picked his ax up and staggered to his feet to rejoin the battle.

"The pitch! Get the pitch on it!" Sinbad cried as he delivered a back cut to the monsters hand when it came too close. Perhaps the boiling resin would have some effect upon the thing.

On the rear deck Al-Hazred heard Sinbad's cry. Hastily went to the cauldron of burning coals and spotted the pot of boiling pine resin. Struck by inspiration he quickly added a handful of Black Lotus flowers he had taken from the lotus jungle and began to chant a primal prayer in ancient Hyborian. The black lotus petals became small and crinkled as he stirred the mixture with his knife blade. The pitch became clear and amber colored even though still boiling and began smoking with a sickening stench. He dropped his knife as the mixture bit into the blade like acid.

Sinbad looked back for a way to get to the aft deck without getting his head torn off when he saw Al-Hazred walking towards them. The otherworldly scholar carried the smoking red hot cauldron of pitch in his bare hands. His gaze was far off as if he was in a dream and he heeded not the press of men or the roar of the monster. Words with no form poured from his lips. "Give the man room!" Sinbad shouted as he urged Ralf and the rest out of the fray after creating some space by the god.

Sthaggua paused a moment to sniff the air and his ears twitched with curiosity at what was brought before him. As he leaned close Al-Hazred tossed the boiling contents of the cauldron in the monsters face.

The toad god screamed in primal pain and fury. Whirling it attempted to clear its eyes and mouth of the burning sticky mass, knocking Al-Hazred down the gang way in to the hold. The creature turned its back on Sinbad and the crew to stagger as if drugged over to the rail. "Now's our chance!" yelled Sinbad. With spears and oars the men pushed it and with a mighty heave it fell over the side into the sea. It lolled in the waves and began to drift back towards its island prison as if some magnetic force drew it back to its lair. The island was rapidly sinking beneath the waves.

"He is beaten!" Omar cried as he gave silent thanks to Allah.

The crew collected themselves from the scattered and cluttered deck to regain control of the ship. The Satrap's ship was heading towards them. Between a raging whirl of water from the islands passing and the enemy ship they had few options. They would either be sucked to the bottom or boarded by the yellow clad killers on the other ship.

"Put us along their port side!" Sinbad cried. "I tire of fighting on our decks." Rolf looked up from his pained ribs with a gleam in his sea rover eyes. He staggered to his feet with ax in hand. It had been a while since he had raided a ship but he would be damned to Helheim if he would miss it today.

Tishimi, Rolf and Henri assembled at the rail next to Sinbad. "We board, we disable her and then we leave. I'll not be looking over my shoulder at every port for the Satrap and his fanatics for the rest of my days." The warriors nodded and checked their weapons.

"Grapples ready! We pass her to starboard!" Omar called as he tugged a sheet tight to put the final touch on their turn for the pass.

"Turn wide as you pass and then come back for us. Sinbad drew his dagger and paused before he placed it in his teeth. "Mind the whirlpool, but do not put the ship at risk if you cannot get us."

"We will be there Captain." he grunted, seeing the increasing swell of water that tugged at the ships course from the maelstrom forming where the island used to be. The deck smelled of blood, pitch and sea spray as the Blue Nymph rode to battle.

By now the Satrap's men had begun to organize and fight back the fire that had already decimated their sails. Several of his warrior sent arrows that went hissing into the sea as the Blue Nymph bore down on its quarry. They charged each other in a seaborne joust and four grapples flew true. The Blue Nymph pulled by at half and oars length distance. Sinbad and his companions grabbed the lines and swung over the intervening space to bring mayhem on the enemy's deck. With a clatter of ropes and grapples the ships almost kissed sides and then parted.

Henri landed in one of the few undamaged sails still in the rigging. He rode its curve down to the deck to land on his feet. Like a striking falcon he drew his sword and sliced through some of the stays holding the canvas firm against the wind. The whole thing began to flap uselessly as a half dozen of the yellow clad killers moved at him with daggers and swords drawn. Henri smiled. He preferred the bow but his arm needed a warm up before he feathered his way through these motherless sons. Striking engarde he parried a dagger stroke and stabbed the man in the foot with his sword, followed by a crushing blow to his opponents jaw with the hilt. He engaged the rest in a play of blades but the fanatics were stymied by his fighting style from half a world away.

With a crash amidships one of the yardarms stood bent at an odd angle. When he landed, Rolf had hit it but miraculously had no enemies about him! Cursing his luck and sore head he buried his ax in the mainmast. The mighty wood shivered and a flicker of strategy was born in his fighting mad brain. Like a man possessed he attacked the wooden mast over and over as if it was a troll from his homeland. The few assassins who tried to close with him to stop his destruction were brained by the flashing arc of razor steel as Rolf was adept in using his back swing while he fought.

One came too close and the battle ax bit deep into his chest with a spout of gore. Shaking the man loose as a woodsman would a stray chip on his axehead, Rolf landed a final mighty blow on his wooden foe. The main mast cracked like a thunder stroke and snapped sideways falling across the deck of the ship to lie half dragging in the sea. It had carried some of the enemy crew over the side in its tangled heap of lines and shrouds. The whole mess began to affect the ship's course like a sea anchor and the craft began spiraling to port.

Henri came through the debris from forward, his bow strung but his crimsoned sword still in hand. He looked in amazement at what the giant Norseman had done. "Mon Dieu! That was the greatest feat of felling I have ever seen!" He covered his companion as the Viking recovered his wind.

Rolf stood from catching his breath and paused to retrieve his fallen sword. The enemy began to pour onto the deck from below. "Not really. I was trying to get it to fall to the bow," he grinned.

Suddenly he and Henri were in pitched close combat. Several of the fanatics charged forward with curved swords flashing. Henri danced back and warded off their initial strike with a flourish. He ran the first man through his chest.

Sinbad climbed down through the bowels of the ship. He had landed near an unguarded hatchway and intended to make the most of it. The place was a shambles and the stench was horrendous. The crew's bunks lay empty. Sinbad quickly made his way to the lowest point he could find. Grabbing a sheet, some oakum and hemp cordage he made a pile and smashed a lantern to it. The flames began to rise and the dark chamber was briefly lit. It looked like a scene from a nightmare. There was blood everywhere and a strange symbol was repeated over and over on makeshift banners and the walls were clotted with the gore of past sacrifices. Sinbad steeled himself and went up a nearby gangway to the upper decks. Sitting at the wheel was an evil looking half caste dressed in yellow who drew a pair of katars and rushed him. Behind the man was the Satrap himself.

Sinbad dodged a pair of blade filled fists as he wove a web of his own steel. "Why doesn't your master fight? Is he but a coward who only works puppets to his will?" The Saffron Satrap stood motionless by the fantail his burning black eyes the only part of his face visible from his tattered and cloth swathed form. The man parried his counter attack expertly and would not rise to Sinbad's baiting.

The pilot gathered himself, "The master is above all life good and evil. He will have the apostate as a sacrifice and use your ship as a scow for slaves. Nothing you do can stop him. He is The Unspeakable Word made flesh! *Ia! Ia! Hastur ambulati!*" The man's attacks were good and Sinbad found himself backing away as he tried to stretch the distance between them.

The pilot dove to tackle Sinbad to the ground where he could gut him with his knives. Sinbad leaped over his rush with the grace of a lifetime of jumping and moving on rigging. The cultist slipped to his knees and Sinbad ran him neatly through at the junction of his neck and shoulder from behind. The man was dead before he hit the deck in an unmoving heap.

Sinbad extricated his blade from the guard as he watched the Satrap. The tall gaunt figure made no move to a weapon or the free spinning wheel that steered the ship; he simply stared at the captain of the Blue Nymph with those dead eyes. Sinbad caught himself falling into their gaze. It was as if the lifeless cold of the space in the night sky looked back at him. He heard the Satrap's voice as if from far away and he could not move his limbs.

"Your sword will avail you not, man of Sindh. I am the unseen walker in the wastes. I have died and lived in a thousand forms and eras. My step is the tread of doom upon this world and all your efforts cannot thwart me from my task. Your mother's people howled at my altars in the dim past and your father's ancestors died on them. Sacrifice yourself to me."

Unbelievably Sinbad felt his arms raise his sword to his own breast. By some foul sorcery his limbs were not his own to command!

Suddenly a lightning stroke of unbelievable power split the clouds overhead. It briefly illuminated Tishimi crouching unseen on the rail. Her blue fire tinged sword flashed in a diagonal cut from heaven to earth as she split the Satraps body from shoulder to hip. As the tattered figure fell to the ground Sinbad felt his own body snap back under his control. Whatever power the Satrap had held him in momentarily was gone.

Tishimi shook her head to clear her ears of seawater. She was soaked to the bone from her inadvertent missing of the rear of the ship on the boarding action. They looked at the rag covered remains on the deck. Perhaps it was the light or the rocking sea but they both felt ill if they looked at the strange corpse for too long. Neither wanted to touch it. "He talked too much." Tishimi grunted.

"With such power, no wonder his men cast their lives away with abandon." Sinbad nodded. "We must go!"

Sinbad looked forward and saw Henri and Ralf making their way aft. They appeared to be none the worse for wear. Scanning the horizon he searched for the Blue Nymph through the haze and storm as the fire in the hold below began to eat away at the ships guts like a hungry hyena. The Blue Nymph, with Omar at the wheel, was a mile off and had started to make a run towards their burning ship.

The cultists damaged vessel was starting to turn uncontrollably as it began to be swept towards the whirlpool. With her sails aflame, Sinbad knew the rudder was their only chance now. He grabbed the wheel to try and check the vessels yawing. The helm spun loosely. Tishimi cursed. "I cut the rudder chain on the way up."

"Rope! As long as you can find, quickly!" Sinbad took a sighting on the Blue Nymph as it lined up to pass. It was going to be close and they only had one shot at this. Ralf and Henri dragged a coil of rope to the rail. There was no way Henri's bow would be able to carry the end of this line to the passing ship, not on his best day.

"Tie the line around yourselves at intervals. We weight the end and toss it to be caught by the Blue Nymph when she passes close. Omar will know to secure it and pull us in." Sinbad began rigging a loop around himself and soon the others were also tied on.

Ralf tied a large knot in the end of the line to give it some weight for throwing. He quickly counted off how many fathoms of rope were left in the length. The Blue Nymph had better come very close indeed. "When I throw it, wait a moment and then jump in. It will give them time to secure it. "Sinbad cautioned them. Tishimi knotted cords around her weapons so as not to lose them in the water, and the others did the same. Sinbad stood on the rail and waved to the Blue Nymph. The ocean between them churned like a stirred cauldron.

Omar threw the rudder over and ordered the sail trimmed to adjust their course slightly. There would only be one chance at this. The other ship was aflame now and he could see figures on the stern. "Haroun, are they there?"

The eagle eyed waif called down from the most hazardous place on the ship. "Aye! The Captain and the others are on the aft port rail. They are readying a line! They mean to throw it over I think." He hurried down the mast to the deck before Omar could tell him it was too dangerous.

Omar bellowed, "All hands watch for that toss! If it doesn't snag, make it fast. We'll pass them to starboard!" He lined up the run and saw that other ship was burning fully now. This maneuver seemed simple but was very dangerous. Sparks from the one ship could alight the other if it came too close. Not to mention that they had to head into the maelstrom created by the islands passing. He only hoped whoever was piloting the other ship kept its course steady.

Sinbad wound up for the toss, choking back tears as the smoke billowed all around them. He had wound his *shemagh* across his face to protect his lungs but it must not cover his eyes. He saw the Blue Nymph's bow flash by with her never changing smile and tossed for it on the up roll. With the speed the ships were passing he waited two quick breaths and then flung himself into the sea. The rest followed after to avoid having their backs snapped when the line went taught.

The knotted line crashed onto the deck of the Blue Nymph and skidded towards the stern with the crew chasing and diving after it like children in some demented game. It hung for a moment on a splintered stanchion left from the rampaging gods destruction and then Haroun grabbed it with both hands and set a loop of its slack about a stay. The rest of the deck crew began to secure the line. At that moment the load of the captain and his party hit the rope. It thrummed like the plucked string of a Sitar but held fast without parting.

Omar turned the ship away from the churning water on a course to safety. "Haul them in!" Al-Hazred and the rest of the free crew started to drag the line up the side bringing the four wayward crew and captain aboard. They were soaked to the bone and all had lost their shoes and Sinbad even his shirt.

They lay gasping on the deck for a moment as it had been a near thing.

"Get us out of here, due North." Sinbad ordered as he made his weary way to the pilot house. Henri and Tishimi tended to Ralf's wounds and blankets were brought up to keep them warm. Being towed through the water had been like being dragged though snow so great was its ability to suck the heat from a body.

Sinbad could see the flaming enemy ship gaining speed and heading away to the crushing eye of the maelstrom's vortex. As it passed closer on its round about journey to a watery doom Sinbad thought he saw a shape swathed in yellow tatters and wreathed in by flames. The shape's gaze never wavered from the Blue Nymph even as the swirling waters closed over the ship dragging it to whatever watery hell it would lay in forever. He turned and realized Al-Hazred was standing near him and had seen it as well.

The scholar's desperate expression was a terrible sight to behold.

After another week of good winds the Blue Nymph finally came to port in Bengali. She was made fast to her slip so her passenger could disembark. Many of the crew were anxious to get on dry land after so long a voyage without a port. They had traded a few of the less fantastic pearls with passing ships for food and water.

Henri was already looking for the greatest concentration of beautiful women in close proximity to wine and gambling. Omar had a long list of supplies and repairs he needed to tend to at port so they would lay over for a day or two perhaps. Tishimi was re-wrapping and re-oiling her sword as she had been for a week to keep rust at bay after the drenching they both had received. Ralf stood near the figurehead on the bow. He was fully armed and armored in his warrior's best to strike fear into the hearts of any port rats. He saw the advantage of spreading the legend of 'Captain Sinbad's killer giant from the north.'

Sinbad walked Al-Hazred to the gang way to shore. He smiled at the spring in his crew's step as they were on land again. By the end of the week they would set off to better waters to sell their treasures. Chatgaon was too rich in pearls for the booty to bring a good price so they would have to sail elsewhere to avoid flooding the market. Also he must find men who would fill the vacant spots in his crew. There were good sailors to be found here. They must be, to replace the good ones he had lost.

"Thank you Captain, I was only looking for a safe passage to the east but you have helped me to learn even more about my chosen field of study. Mayhap I can now travel to some far off places I have heard about here, even beyond to the furthest eastern shores." Al-Hazred fished about in his pack and produced a scroll. He handed it to Sinbad. "A gift, not a treasure map to gold but some poetic musings of an old scholar. Think of me kindly when you read it. Goodbye, Captain Sinbad" He raised his hand and salaamed deeply and turned to go.

"Fare well Al-Hazred." The Arab was off on a dark and lonesome path. Sinbad's glance wavered as the mad scholar walked off the Blue Nymph and disappeared into the crowd. He appeared headed towards the caravanserai to find passage overland.

Sindbad looked over the opened scroll and was amazed at the calligraphy and marginal artwork depicting some of the fantastic things they had seen on the journey. Clearly the master scholar had slaved over it for the weeks they had been at sea. He read the scrip therein to himself as he went back to his cabin. 'That is not dead which can eternal lie...'

On the docks a group of huddled figures watched as Al-Hazred passed by and discussed it in hushed tones.

THE END

The Mad Arab

Much like a character in a story I was gripped by the knowledge of unknown things and drawn forward into madness.

That madness was writing a new pulp tale. I wanted plenty of action for the Sinbad story so I thought long and hard about the source material. Tales of the sea are very old and compelling things. The Pulps abound with stories of mariners both modern and ancient and the lands they travel to. The greatest is easily Sinbad. I remember watching these movies with my father when I was a kid. Swords, monsters and adventure rolled of the screen and into our imaginations. My boyhood held many swash buckling, stick brandishing moments in lieu of actual swords. I found the adventure in everyday life and the wonder of it all kept me going when all wonder usually begins to fade.

It would have to have action! What caused the action in the story was a bit of a stumbler. I went to the source material and read up on the history of the region, the Sindhi sailors, and the gulf waters they plied their trade on. I researched routes from India to Damascus and parts in between.

Damascus. Damascus! Why did that name bug me? They were known for their trade and steel, but were landlocked, being many miles from the sea. Not very good for an adventure involving sailors. What else was it about that ancient city that nagged at my brain?

The Mad Arab! I quickly checked online and in texts. I had to be sure of my information. It was true! Lovecraft's mad scholar of the Cthulhu mythos cycle was from Damascus but he traveled the world for many years. Traveled means caravans and ships and...What if Abdul Al-Hazrad needed to book passage to someplace far away? He was, at best, a heretic in the eyes of the Faithful. One man had a ship, full of foreign sailors and he dared travel anywhere. This would be a story of how they met and what happened after. Once the idea of a meeting between these two took hold the story practically outlined itself.

I knew my sword fighting and knot tying well enough (Ask my wife how we met. Wait, that came out weird.), but I really needed to bone up on my seamanship, especially rope and marlin spike sailing. Research cleared up the details for the sea battles and the technical details of reefing or handling a ship. The mythos and monsters details I tried to keep simple and within the framework of the genre. I tried to work in a nice homage to all the other authors past and present who use the magical Lotus flowers in the pulps by having the island be where they all originally came from. It seemed fitting that such a powerful narcotic be used to keep the dread god asleep.

The toughest part of the whole process was finding the right mix of soul numbing horror and devil may care action. At first glance these would seem to be mutually exclusive, but by having everyone in the crew relate to elements of the mythos they might have brushed upon, it made their world bump up against the more terrifying and soul numbing one of Al-Hazrad himself. This helped to produce a lurking dread but not an overwhelming one for our heroes to defeat.

Special thanks to Ron of course. Your love of these stories is a true compass for lost mariners in search of adventure. Stay the course! To my 'beta readers' Andy and Kevin I salute you as fellow adventurers. Your help was greatly appreciated to put this beast to rest. Lastly to my family: my wife Lisa and daughter Honor, and my Mom and Dad. Because you cant wander far from home if you don't have something to go back to at journeys end.

JEFF FOURNIER - Jeff Fournier is an Ohio native who has been writing fiction and non-fiction stories since he was in college. An avid reader of Science Fiction and Fantasy he discovered Robert E. Howard and H.P. Lovecraft early on and was a fan of the stories they spun. Later he went to University as an Art/Illustration major where he worked with others at school writing and drawing for a shared universe super hero 'zine called *Vanguard Dossier.* After school he married his fiance Lisa and went on to work in the field of Private Investigations and Contract Security. The 'Venture' nickname came from his favorite 'go to' fake name when dealing with unsavory types in investigations long past. Jeff can be found on Facebook at https://www.facebook.com/jeff.venture.1

In his spare time he has tried to keep his hand in various creative outlets, writing non-fiction articles for SJ Games *Pyramid, Self-Reliance Illustrated,* and working on designing things in Kydex and canvas for the outdoors. This is his first Story for Airship 27.

Sinbad & the Rakshasa's Gambit

by I.A. Watson

R ed sands trickled through the hourglass' neck. The maiden picked up an ivory pawn and advanced it two squares. "Shah's infantry to shah four." The game had begun.[1]

She swiveled the glass so that the sands fell in reverse. Now it was Sinbad's time that drained away through the bottleneck, grain by grain.

"Who are you?" the sailor asked the veiled damsel. She was beautiful, he could tell, for her almond skin was smooth and unblemished and her green eyes shone. Long black tresses were filleted with silver, coiling behind her almost to the floor. Her hands were deft and slender, her deli-

---

1   King's pawn to king 4.

The names of chess pieces have varied considerably during the game's long history. The Indian game of *shatranj* anticipated king, queen, bishop, knight, rook, and pawn with shah, wazir, elephant, horseman, chariot, and infantry. Although the moves were somewhat different in early versions of the game this story assumes that the current rules have developed, even the two-square pawn opening. The most significant development that Sinbad encounters in this game is that the wazir, a weak piece which could only move one square diagonally, has been replaced by the queen with her wide-ranging powers. For more discussion on the matter see the afternote.

Ways of describing chess moves have likewise evolved, from poetical lengthy descriptions in Shakespeare's time to modern algebraic notation. The characters in our present story use classic descriptive notation, in which each refers to ranks (rows) counting from his or her side of the board and columns by the piece that uses it as a starting position. This notation was common until the end of the 20th century and is still preferred by some older traditionalists.

This story hereafter mostly translates the names of the pieces to their modern English counterparts for ease of reading, as it translates other dialogue from Sinbad's native tongue.

cate nails varnished with the faintest tint. Her belly, exposed by the two-piece harem outfit she wore, was flat and sensuous. Behind her translucent gauze covering, her lips looked full and inviting.

"I may not say," she answered the question. "Play the game, stranger."

Sinbad matched her move exactly and flipped the timer. "King's pawn to the fourth rank," he announced. "I'm Sinbad, by the way. Sinbad el Ari, sailing out of Baghdad, city of marvels."

"I didn't ask," answered the maiden. She moved her king's knight out to the third rank in front of her bishop. "I try not to know the names of the men I kill."

"Well I want you to remember mine," Sinbad insisted. "After all, if I'm going to lose this chess match and die for it, I'd like to think that I'd be remembered by a beautiful lady afterwards. Vizier's knight to third rank, vizier's bishop's column."

"It's not a vizier in this version of the game," the maiden insisted. "She is the *rani*, a queen, and she is the most powerful of the pieces." She slid her bishop out diagonally to the fourth rank, commanding the middle of the board.

Sinbad sat back and folded his arms. "If you won't tell me who you are, at least tell me how you came to be here," he pleaded. "Why do you insist on playing chess with your prisoners and killing them if they lose?"

The damsel frowned at him. "That's not my choice. I don't set the rules of the game. That is my captor's choice."

"You're a prisoner too?" Sinbad noticed the elegant silver bands on her wrists and neck. They were gorgeous expensive slave chains but they were slave chains all the same.

"Of course I am captive. It is not only my opponent who dies if he loses."

Sinbad had been about to move a piece. His hand halted over the board. "Wait a moment... Are you saying that if I lose then my life is forfeit, but if you lose then you die instead?"

"That is the game, yes. If you fail, you are devoured alive. If I lose, it is I who am torn apart and eaten...eventually. And if we reach stalemate, or return to the same formation three times, or simply refuse to play, then we will both die. Make a move now, please."

Sinbad tried to remember how he came to be here, in this high tower, its bulb minaret open at each cardinal point to balconies that overlooked wide green lands below. Northwards and south ran a spine of mountains. The palace and its tower topped the highest peak. A snaking river ran eastwards to a glittering sea, sparkling under a morning sun. The sailor thought he recognized the tiny islets of Nagadiba and Zibala, which meant he must be on the much larger isle of Lanka; but he could see no city in the lush jungle below, or sign of habitation at all.

The chamber he and the maiden occupied was luxurious but unusual. The walls were of brass, formed into delicate and elaborate scrollwork, twisted columns knotting and combining into a spherical tower-top some forty feet across. Now that Sinbad considered it again, the structure reminded him of some pretty bird-cage, but a cage all the same.

Shelves and pedestals were strewn with rich treasures. The silk curtains, the silver dishes filled with fruit and sweetmeats, the soft cushions and thick carpets failed to hide that there seemed no exit from the room. The only escape would be a plunge from those graceful balconies to the harsh rocks beneath.

Sinbad slid his own king's bishop out to his fourth rank, to stand beside hers. "So... how did I get here?" he wondered. "I was on the *Blue Nymph*, my ship, you should see her, she's a beauty too, making for Tarshish to trade copper for ivory. There was a strange fog-bank and... then a creature. It just appeared on deck, man-sized and shaped, but tiger-headed and cat-tailed. Green fire burned from his paws and eyes. He roared. My comrades took up arms. One almost reached him before... I don't know. The fog thickened, moved in, choked us."

The sailor searched his memories of those confused blurred moments. He thought he remembered Tishimi dropping to deck mere paces from her enemy, and Henri behind her struggling to draw back his bow before falling prey to the mist. Had Sinbad uncoiled a rope and swung in from the prow at the monster, only to have it catch him by the throat with supernatural reflex? Soreness and scratches at the hero's neck now suggested perhaps he had.

There were other impressions too, vivid but disjointed: a palace filled with servants of colored glass, walking statues who attended to their fierce cat-headed master; a fountain of blood where the monster dipped a jeweled goblet for a celebratory quaff; a library jammed with scrolls and books where the creature had picked up quill and inscribed Sinbad's name for his records; a twisted spiral stair of smoke towards this tower prison.

Sinbad looked over to the maiden in her gossamer robes of purple and gold, with her dazzling, frightened eyes. "And finally there was you, here. Playing chess."

The captive beauty nudged the pawn before her queen's bishop a space forward to stand behind her king's bishop. "Each of the opponents against whom I have played arrived here on Butterfly Mountain[2] without knowing how he came. Our captor has powerful magics, illusions that can baffle the senses; and his instincts are cruel."

"I don't suppose you'll tell me who he is?"

"He calls himself Rukh Bakasur, master of the isle of Taprobana."

Sinbad frowned. "Taprobana is an old name for Lanka, for Ceylon."[3] He looked beyond to tower at the thick forest below. "I had expected to see more settlement."

The maiden nodded gracefully. She did everything gracefully. "I think... I believe that we are in some different place to the destination for which you sailed, some other island, like the one men have tamed but wild and magical, existing alongside that other like two twins in a single womb. If one brother will strangle the other before birth I cannot say. Certain, though, that this is Bakasur's realm and all in it are his playthings."

"I'm not feeling that playful," Sinbad admitted. "So our host's called Bakasur. What is he? A tiger transformed to a man or a man cursed to be a tiger?"

The maiden shuddered. "He is a Rakshasa, one of the demon spirits that haunt this corner of the world. Like the fallen djinni *ghuls* of the waste places beyond Baghdad, in the haunted ruins of Babel? Masters of magic and illusion with a taste for mortal blood. Tales are told how the rakshasas tried to devour their creator, for they are flesh-eaters and man-eaters; their joy and lust is for slaughter." The captive sighed. "But they are subtle too, and enjoy playing with their food."

Sinbad jumped his other cavalry piece into play. "King's knight to the third rank, king's bishop's column. So I guess I need to rescue you, then?"

The maiden's brows rose. "Rescue me? No-one can rescue me. I am cursed to captivity. I must remain here, killing men until one is cleverer

---

2   The conical mountain in southern Sri Lanka is variously named Samanalakanda ("butterfly mountain" in Singhalese), Sivanolipatha Malai (Tamil), and Sri Pada; the latter name, "sacred footprint", refers to a rock formation near the summit which Buddhists, Hindus, Christians and Moslems variously attribute as the tread of Buddha, Shiva, Adam, or St Thomas. At 7,359 feet it is the most prominent geographical feature of the island. Its southern slopes are the source of rich veins of gems for which the land became famous in medieval times.

3   This is disputed by modern scholars. The name comes from Greek geographer Megasthenes around 290 B.C. and then by Claudius Ptolemy also described a large island south of continental Asia. By the 16th century, beautiful maps such as the one in *Cosmographia Claudii Ptolomaei Alexandrini* detailed an island much like Sri Lanka and tradition identified the island with Ptolemy's Taprobane. Other commentators prefer Taprobana to have been Sumatra or some phantom island.

than me, and then it is I who shall be destroyed by the Rakshasa." She considered the board carefully, but hesitated before making another move.

"You've clearly not heard of me, then," Sinbad told her. "Impossible rescues and daring getaways are the sort of thing I do all the time. I'd tell you some amazing stories if we weren't on the hourglass. Roof-jumping. Monster-fighting. Roc-riding. Really top-class swashbuckling, very impressive." He winked at the girl. "As it is, you'll just have to take my word for it that I'm pretty good. If anyone can get you out of here, it's me."

The maiden hissed and slammed her queen's infantryman two squares forward. That set it threatening both Sinbad's elephant and his pawn. Things were about to get messy. "I told you, you *can't* save me. I'm cursed to slavery. And I warn you I don't want to lose, because although the Rakshasa will tear you apart and feast on your meat he would do far worse to me before I perish." She shuddered.

"That's the second time you've mentioned a curse," the sailor noted. "How did you come to be this Bakasur's prisoner?" He strained his knowledge of languages. "Rakshasa comes from root words meaning... carry off? Or hungry? Or greedy?"

"All of those," replied the maiden. "And ravisher, of course. The people of these islands and the ivory lands to the north speak of a rakshasa marriage when they mean a woman is taken by force. Rakshasa's enjoy devouring everything, and innocence best of all."

"You're not saying how you came to be here. Or have you been forbidden to tell me that as you're not able to tell me your name?"

The maiden shrugged. "What's the point of talking? One of us will die soon. Let's just get on and find out who."

Sinbad tapped the running hourglass. "That's exactly why we should talk. This might be our last conversation. I've always rather hoped my last chat would be with a gorgeous lady and let me tell you how well you qualify! So look, here we are, in an elegant setting with a spectacular view, green and black grapes in silver dishes beside us, cool freshly-squeezed juice in this crystal decanter. Let's at least *enjoy* our last few moments, eh? And perhaps you would tell me your story?"

The maiden eyed the sailor. Was that a twinkle in her appraising gaze? "You are very convincing, Sinbad el Ari. Do women usually fall in love with you at this point? You would have to work a lot harder to win me."

"I'm not known for failing when I try to achieve something."

"There is always a first time, and for one or us today, a last." The maiden smoothed back her midnight locks. "A short story, then. My father's favorite was I, raised by him in noblest degree. From him I learned music and astrology, lore, statecraft, etiquette and justice; all the arts and skills to be his heiress, for the man I wedded would have ruled after him. Others were jealous of my accomplishments and of his choice, and so a curse was prepared and a dark bargain struck. An evil *ghul* carried me away by night. I was placed under a spell of eternal servitude, never to rule, always enslaved. Then I was sold into bondage, and this Rakshasa bid the highest. Since then I have been his captive and I have played his game." The maiden glanced at the hourglass. "Your sands have reached their final grains."

Sinbad took her threatening pawn with his own and flipped the glass. He felt a twinge of guilt, as if he'd dragged the damsel he played against a step closer to the execution block.

He decided on a different gambit. "I wasn't alone on the *Blue Nymph* when that fog surrounded us. I don't suppose you have any idea what this Rakshasa might have done with my comrades?" It wasn't enough for the sailor to escape any more. He'd vowed not to leave any more crew behind either. And then there was this lady…

"This ship of yours," the maiden considered, "A neat little Persian vessel with striped sail and a nymph figurehead?"

"Yes! How do you know?"

The mystery girl rose from the cushions where she sat. Sinbad was able to appreciate her form, lithe and sinuous, thin-waisted but full a hip and breast. She moved like a dancer.

She pointed to a cabinet where a big bell-jar stood atop a silver salver. A model ship bobbed on a miniature sea inside the glass vessel. It looked exactly like the *Blue Nymph*.

"That's an amazing replica!" Sinbad admitted. He went over to examine it closer…and froze.

There were figures on the model's deck and they were moving. As the sailor stared down through the glass he could see Ralf waving back to him. The tiny Norseman pointed up, directing Omar and Henri's attention to the vast face that loomed above them.

"That's not a model, is it?" Sinbad gasped.

The maiden elected not to capture the pawn that had taken her piece, but instead moved the pawn on her fourth king's rank to the fifth, where it was covered by her knight and threatened Sinbad's.

"I warned you he was powerful," she said. "Usually a traveler's companions die when he does. That makes his failure all the more painful. As I said, the Rakshasa enjoys cruel games."

"That's not a model, is it?"

Sinbad saw a crystal trickle from the maiden's eye. How many opponents she had sat across this board from, knowing that only accomplishing their destruction would save her from ravishment, torture, and death?

He jumped his threatened knight forwards to his king's fifth rank. It was a bold gambit that left him vulnerable but gave him options. It was a very Sinbad move.

The maiden went on speaking, more to herself than to her opponent. "When I was first made to play I wondered if I should deliberately lose. Resign, or just play badly. I could not bear the idea of my victory causing the murder of another. What right had I, I asked myself, to save my virtue and my life at such dear cost?"

She advanced her bishop one diagonal forward to her queen's fifth rank, directly between Sinbad's two cavalry-pieces, menacing both. The rearmost was protected by his row of pawns; its capture would be avenged. That questing knight he had ventured outwards had no such cover.

"Then I realized that no matter what I did, the Rakshasa's game would continue. Some other would bear the guilt of survival because I had not the spirit to resist. I determined to struggle. I chose not to yield to the tiger, because surrender is far worse than coercion, and I will not be a coward. So, you see, bold Sinbad the Sailor, I will have to destroy you because there is no victory ever in the Rakshasa's game."

Sinbad would not retreat. He pressed his threatened knight onwards, to the seventh rank in the column of the king's bishop. Now he bracketed two powerful white pieces. His next move could capture either the king's rook or the queen herself.

"I'd prefer not to be destroyed," he admitted. "I'm right with you on the fighting back idea."

"Then you need to choose your battles more carefully," the maiden warned him. She moved her king diagonally forward and took his attacking horseman. "And you need to look more carefully before you leap."

"Not my style," the sailor smiled ruefully. "King's pawn to queen's bishop six, takes your queen's bishop's pawn. Discovered check from my bishop. Surely you see the problem with looking carefully when you've already told me the Rakshasa is a master of illusion? If we can't believe our eyes, if my friends and ship aren't really trapped in a tiny bottle over there and we're not atop a high tower overlooking the whole isle of Taprobana, then we have to go with our instincts. What do your instincts tell you, beautiful and mysterious stranger?"

"They tell me you are very dangerous, Sinbad el Ari. I have been trained to discern the station and worth of men by their manners and motions, by their hands and eyes. And I perceive you are no humble merchant or mere sailor."

Sinbad held out his hands, palm up, and stared into those green irises. "Read me then. What am I?"

The maiden turned from the board where she was unexpectedly in check and smoothed fingertips over the sailor's palms. "A sailor, for certain. Ropes and fish-hooks and weathering, that's plain. But no mere boatman. A captain, by your demeanor, how you naturally assume command, and by your concern for your crew. A traveler, by your confidence in foreign places. A swordsman, by these calluses, but not one who delights in blood, I think. Acrobat, lock-picker, smooth-talker, hard-trader, a cunning survivor who has sometimes regretted survival."

"That is… very perceptive," Sinbad confessed.

"There's more. Underneath the bold façade and those scabs of old regret, what's this? A poet? A visionary? A delighter in old tales and far horizons? And beneath that…" Her eyes widened.

"What else, beauty?"

"A dreamer. A man with a destiny. And inside even that a loving heart. A hero's heart. Oh." She dropped his hands as if they burned her. "I knew you were dangerous to me! You could be my downfall." She shifted her king diagonally forward to the third rank of the king's knight's column, where her horseman shielded it.

"If you are cursed and captive I'd say you've already fallen down," the adventurer pointed out. "Why don't you let me pick you up?"

"Are you really offering to help me? Or are you distracting me so you can defeat me?"

"I'm trying to help."

"Help me? How do you know that I'm not merely another of the Rakshasa's illusions, a pleasing shape to keep you occupied while he weaves his traps about you? Or perhaps I'm a rakshasi myself, a female of that demon race?[4] You don't know what I might conceal beneath these veils."

"I'd love to find out," Sinbad admitted. "I keep thinking that you seem familiar. It's bothering me. And yet we've never met?"

4   That would be a Manushiya-Rakshasi, a human-shaped rakshasa female. In ancient literature they tended to either seduce heroes to their doom or else fall in love with them and aid them in the end. The Mahabharata (Book I: Adi Parva, Section 154) describes how cannibal rakshasa Hidimba sent his sister Hidimbi to spy out his enemy Bhima; instead she fell for the hero, warned him, and saved his life. Hidimbi bore Bhima a half-rakshasa son, Ghatotkacha, who plays in important and prominent part supporting his father in the climactic Kurukshetra war.

"I am certain I would remember," the maiden assured him. She tapped the hourglass. "Your sands are still running out."

Sinbad had one infantry piece far out beyond all the others, with no defense. If he advanced it a square then the white queen could claim it. If he left it where it was then an enemy pawn would take it. He shifted the valiant ebony piece to his queen's knight's seven row, capturing a white infantryman so the pawn could go out in a blaze of glory.

"I'm serious about saving you, if you'd let me," Sinbad told the maiden. "There are ways to break any curse. Slaves can be set free. Captives can return home to families who grieve for them."

"I cannot. I was auctioned in the great souk of the City of Brass. Bakasur bought me with pearls and rubies torn from mortals he had destroyed, and with certain caged souls of children he had consumed. Whatever I was once, I am now his chattel. Almost entirely."

"Almost?"

"Almost. He cannot ravage me until I surrender to him, or else am defeated by some enemy at the game of traps we play today. There is... my curse is complicated. That prevents the Rakshasa's vile touch. So far."

She pursed her lips beneath her wispy veil and determined not to show weakness any more. Her queen's bishop ruthlessly eliminated Sinbad's aggressor pawn. She glared at him aggressively.

"You do play well," the Sailor confessed. "Where did you learn?"

"My father taught me. Nobody beats him at the game, even when he plays it with nations." She fell silent then, worried that she had revealed too much.

Sinbad withdrew his remaining knight to the king's second rank, sealing the only gap in the row of pawns, fortifying the king against intrusion. He had lost a knight and a pawn. The maiden was down four of her pawns but had taken no other losses. She advanced her knight to king's knight five. Sinbad jumped his own horseman forward again, to queen four, leaving the girl's forward knight open to capture by his newly-revealed black queen.

"She *is* the most dangerous adversary," Sinbad agreed. "While you're pondering what to do, pass me your hands. It's my turn to see what I can read."

The maiden reluctantly showed her palms. She shuddered as Sinbad stroked them. "These fingers have played the harp and lyre. They have weaved and sewn. You have written too, which is a rare accomplishment. They are very fair but not flawless, which is why I don't believe you are rakshasi or illusion. Your eyes mask your fear with a blazing spirit. You are certainly noble, of the highest degree. Virtuous, honest, wise beyond your years…" He paused as she had before, as his insights took him deeper. "Kind beyond measure. Hurt by the deaths you have seen. Subtle, intelligent, brilliant perhaps, passionate in all things."

The maiden snatched her hands hastily, wiping them on her harempants as if to scrub Sinbad off them. She grabbed her forward knight and captured the black king's bishop's pawn, slamming the piece down to threaten queen and rook, to tempt his king out to take the piece so her own queen might come into play. She was, as the sailor had perceived, subtle and brilliant.

"I think we have seen enough of one another now, Sinbad el Ari," she told him.

"No," replied the sailor. "Sometimes partnering is the only way to survive." He castled, sheltering away his king while his rook menaced the attacking knight.

"I'm sorry," the maiden told him. "You lose your queen." She lifted her knight and removed Sinbad's most powerful piece from the board.

Sinbad swooped his king's bishop down all the way to king's bishop seven. "Oh, you know how it is," he grinned. "You lose a queen, you find a princess. Check."

The maiden blanched. "What do you mean?" She retreated her king to king's rook three.

Sinbad advanced his queen's pawn a space forward so the white king was in discovered check from his bishop. "I noticed how familiar you seem with Baghdad and the ruins beyond. So you'd know that a little while ago the Caliph's favorite daughter was carried away by a wicked *ghul*. The kidnapper took her shape and pretended to be her. There was a whole plot to kill Haroun al Rashid; I foiled it brilliantly.[5] But the missing princess was never discovered."

The maiden advanced her pawn to king six, where it was protected by her knight and blocked the bishop's line to her king. Her hand trembled. "Haroun… the Caliph… he is safe? He is saved?"

"Yes. Although there were some awkward loose ends regarding a missing daughter and me in her bedroom. Again. Knight to king's bishop, fifth rank. Another check. You can't tell me who you are, by rakshasa command. Can you nod if I get it right?"

The girl advanced her king diagonally forward. Now it was beside

---

5   See "Sinbad and the Sapphire of the Djinn" by I.A. Watson in *Sinbad: The New Voyages* volume 1.

Sinbad's swashbuckling knight and might eliminate the piece next move. "Don't guess," she pleaded.

"The Caliph of Baghdad's beloved child was Princess Ayesha al Kamineh sitt Anoush; Ayesha the desired, daughter of the immortal. Knight to king three, takes your pawn."

The maiden winced. Her own knight eliminated Sinbad's.

"Well, am I right?" the sailor demanded. "Ayesha." His bishop took her knight in return. "Check."

She advanced her king a square to escape, glaring at her opponent ruefully. "Yes," she confessed, closing her eyes. She knew what would happen now.

There was a stench of raw meat and cat sweat. Sinbad jumped up to see the Rakshasa standing behind him.

"You play the game well, traveler," the cat purred. He folded his arms, rich red robe glistening with golden thread and seeded rubies, striped furred paws with their cruel sheathed claws resting on his elbows. His tiger's head topped Sinbad's, staring down at the sailor with unblinking interest.

"Well enough to bring you to watch," Sinbad responded. "But now you're here, perhaps you can offer a rules clarification."

Bakasur gestured to the ebony and ivory board. "You are here to challenge her, not me."

"That's your game. I'll play it because I must, because you have my ship and my crew, and Ayesha. But it doesn't mean that's the only game I get to play. So what I want to know is what happens if I win?"

"She told you," the Rakshasa replied.

"No. She told me what happens if I lose or she does. If I fail then you torture and devour me. If she fails then you wreak your lust upon her. But what does the winner get? In any wager of chance there's got to be a prize as well as a forfeit."

Barasur seemed amused. "What do you suggest? I've already promised the winner survival to play another day."

"Well yes," agreed Sinbad. "But that's the winner of the game between Ayesha and me. What about the other game, where you've got me trapped between the lady and the tiger? What if I beat *you*? Now there's a wager, if you dare to take it." He swept his rook to the fourth rank, where it was covered by his bishop and covered the maiden's king. "Check again, Ayesha."

The Rakshasa watched the game with interest, calculating moves in advance. He saw the end coming. "A wager requires the wagerer to own something of value. Since I already have you, your ship, your comrades, and the Caliph's daughter, it would seem you have nothing left to hazard."

Sinbad hesitated, struggling for options.

The princess paused. Under her gauze veil she bit her lip. She made a decision. She retreated her king a rank to escape attack. "Rukh Bakasur? Bold Sinbad might have nothing to wager but I still do. There is a prohibition that has prevented you from spoiling me unless I fail your contest. If I win today then I'm protected still. If I fail then I face a miserable end at your pleasure but Sinbad and his people go free. Either outcome allows you cruel sport. But how if I wager my protection that Sinbad el Ari can defeat you? Would that be stakes enough?"

Sinbad looked at Ayesha in awe. "You'd risk that?"

"You're a boaster and a conman, Sinbad el Ari, but you are also a hero, with a good heart. Princesses have duties to heroes. Sometimes we have to save them." She blinked moist eyes and touched Sinbad's chest. "I am tired of being the means of men's downfall. Just once I would like to hazard on a good man so he might survive."

"I accept," snarled the Rakshasa, triumphantly. "You have until the end of the game to defeat me, traveler, and then the wench is mine at last!"

"Hold on," objected Sinbad. "I haven't told you the rest of the stakes. If *I* win, if I beat your game, then me and my crew go free, on the *Blue Nymph*, without any harm. And Ayesha is free too."

"I cannot break the curse of indenture upon her," Bakasur admitted. "It is magic older and stronger than mine."

Sinbad thought quickly. "Then… if I win, she belongs to me. If she must be a slave, then she's my slave."

"What?" exploded the princess. "Why you…!"

"A bargain," agreed the Rakshasa. "You fools."

"*What* did you just pact?" Ayesha fumed at Sinbad.

"A chance," the sailor replied.

"A chance for you, you mean," the maiden scorned. "I see your gambit now. If you win the game with me then you go free. If you somehow overcome the Rakshasa than you go free with me as your toy. Only in defeating you can I endure, in the same vile bondage as before, to murder more strangers as they are brought before me."

"Play on, traveler," Rukh Bakasur demanded. "Your glass is almost done."

"It's the small things that can kill us," Sinbad reflected. He shifted his king's rook's pawn two places ahead, to place Ayesha's king in check again. "The little details that get overlooked."

The maiden blinked miserably at the board. She saw now what was going to happen. Sinbad had sacrificed his queen to kill a princess. What had seemed like a foolish mistake now proved to be the key to victory.

She had only one place to go. She slid her king diagonally back to king's rook three; a single move from checkmate and destruction.

"If… if you return to Baghdad, Sinbad," she asked quietly, "will you please tell my father what became of me? That I tried to do what was right in a situation where there was no right? That I loved him to the end? Let him know that… I tried to be worthy of him."

"You are worthy of him," Sinbad assured her. "I met your lookalike once, the *ghul* who took your shape. She was beautiful and alluring and… not as clothed as you are, but she was *nothing* compared to you. Having seen you now I could never be fooled again. It's the difference between illusion and reality, glamor and substance. She pretended to be noble and fair. You are noble and fair without even thinking about it. If I have to tell anything to Haroun al Rashid, I'll tell him that. But…"

The Rakshasa laid his hand upon the hourglass. The time for Sinbad's final move was running out.

"But?" breathed Ayesha.

"But first I have to defeat Bakasur. There's the matter of a wager."

"How do you propose to do that, bold Sinbad?"

"By ending our game in a way a reaver marauder like him would never think of. You told me the rules, I recall, princess. A penalty for the loser or for both if there was stalemate, time ran out, or moves became repetitive."

"Yes."

"And if a player resigns, knocks over his king and declares the game forfeit?"

"Then he loses, and his life is forfeit too," purred the Rakshasa. "It would not even save the toothsome wench now, for she has wagered her only protection that you will overcome me. Your death would be her downfall too." The tiger-headed monster watched his prisoners with malicious interest. "What I wonder is whether you will now betray her, shattering her tentative desperate hope in you, breaking her heart, and so save yourself; for there is now no chance at all for the Caliph's daughter."

Sinbad ignored the villain. He leaned over and grabbed Ayesha's hands. "Listen, if *one* player resigns he forfeits. What if *both* resign together? It's a draw, but not stalemate or any other thing you mentioned."

"True!" the maiden gasped. "The Rakshasa could never imagine that anyone might work together that way, in mutual trust and sacrifice."

She slid her king diagonally…

"The queen is the most powerful piece on the board," Sinbad reminded her.

"And it supports the king best of all," Ayesha replied.

The last few red grains entered the funnel from the hourglass' upper chamber.

"I'll be your slave then, Sinbad el Ari," Ayesha agreed, "for now. And I will trust you."

Sinbad and the maiden each reached for their kings and toppled them at the same time.

"No!" growled Bakasur. "That is cheating!"

"Actually," Sinbad laughed, "that is winning. Pay up, Rakshasa!"

The tiger-headed demon lunged at him with claws and teeth.

Ayesha hurled herself in the way. Bakasur's thrust tore her flesh, not her hero's. She spun to the ground, bleeding from deep gashes to shoulder and back.

The curse that swathed her heaved like a cloak of shadow as she intercepted the blow. The Rakshasa was hurled away by sorcery more dire than his own, corkscrewed into the side of his rotunda with bone-cracking force.

"Ayesha!" Sinbad cried, stooping to the injured princess at his feet.

She stared up at him, ignoring pain, eyes blazing with the battle-fury of her ancestors. "Get him!" she commanded. "Now, while his magics are thwarted, put him in checkmate!"

Sinbad looked around for a weapon.

"Ignore his illusions, bold Sinbad," the Caliph of Baghdad's daughter insisted. "You were armed on your *Blue Nymph*. You are armed now."

Sinbad found his scimitar hung at his belt as before. The princess spoke only the truth. It was hard to say which weapon was more dangerous.

He leaped at the Rakshasa, flipping over to avoid a lethal claw-swipe, delivering a cut at the monster's collar. Bakasur snarled and snapped his jaws at Sinbad's shoulder. The sailor jinked back so that only the cloth of his tunic ended up between the tiger's teeth.

The Rakshasa was distracted by a chess-board hurled like a discus into the side of his head. Ayesha was up and did not intend Sinbad to fight alone.

The sailor used the diversion and jabbed his blade into the demon's chest. A black blood oozed from the wound but Bakasur swatted Sinbad away. The Rakshasa vanished, leaving the gore-stained scimitar to clatter onto the ground.

No carpet dampened the echo of its fall. The minaret's rich trappings had vanished with the Rakshasa. Now the tower seemed made of bone, stark and bare save for Sinbad, the princess, and the scattered chess-pieces. A cold wind blew through the gaps where the skeletal balconies looked over a bleak and desolate Taprobana.

Sinbad retrieved his weapon and slashed randomly in case an invisible monster lurked close by. Finally he left off and went to check on Ayesha. "How hurt are you?"

The maiden bled from three scratches over shoulder and back. Tattered purple gaze was carmine with her blood. "This is the least of the wounds he has given me," she told Sinbad. "It is mere flesh and blood. If the curse does not heal me then I will carry the scars nobly for a deed well done."

"Well done? Brave, I admit. Foolish perhaps."

"A sacrifice play. Lose the queen but advance the knight, position the enemy to be cornered and beaten. You taught me that. I try to learn fast."

"Indeed you do." Sinbad looked around, but the cabinet that had contained the bottled *Blue Nymph* had vanished with all the other trappings. "I don't suppose you know the way back to my ship? Or even off this tower-top?"

"I'm not a djinn to grant wishes," Ayesha scorned. "Perhaps there's a trap-door? Now that the illusion has gone, or at least peeled back a layer, we might find something?"

Sinbad discovered where the bone slabs hinged open to reveal a spinal stair below. "Let's go. Who know how long Bakasur will be handicapped by crossing your curse?"

They balanced carefully down the spiral of bones, for some steps were still grisly with meat and others crumbled beneath their step. It was a slow, dangerous descent into the halls beneath.

The glass servants that Sinbad had seen before were there, only now they seemed formed of bodily fluids, swirling and oozing as they moved around. They fled from Sinbad and Ayesha's approach.

"Where's the door out?" Sinbad wondered.

"That way," the princess supposed, "behind those skeleton guards?"

The walking skeletons wore antique armor and carried bronze blades. Sinbad skidded down and cut the legs from the first, then whacked the head off a second. It did not stop them from fighting.

As soon as he'd disarmed one, Ayesha took up its shortsword and joined in, covering his back. "Are you surprised that a woman might fight?" she demanded defiantly.

"Nope. Tishimi Osara, a member of my crew, a swordsmith's daughter, she does that stuff all day. Your father really did train you to follow him, didn't he?"

"Tishimi," Ayesha sounded the alien name. "Your woman?"

"My friend. Pay attention to hitting skeletons, princess. No need to be jealous."

"Jealous? I was feeling sorry for her! Duck!"

Sinbad dropped just in time as the maiden swung her sword over his head and decapitated a skeleton that had rushed in on his blind side.

Past the walking bones they found the main doors. A dozen fierce and terrible rakshasa warriors stood between them and freedom.

"Except they are not real," Ayesha revealed. "Show yourself, Rukh Bakasur. We're not playing your games any more. You lost your wager. Let us go or come out and fight!"

"Preferably let us go," Sinbad amended.

"Very well," growled the Rakshasa. The other images vanished, leaving only the tallest and most deadly-looking of the demons. He wore carved battle-armor inlaid with black gems and carried barbed swords in each hand. His tiger-head was covered by a golden helm. "Sometimes the oldest ways are the best. Kill the man, take his woman. Let's play."

"My woman?" Sinbad looked at the princess. She tousled very well, and her imperfections made her more desirable still. "Yes, I suppose she is, since she's technically my property now. Which means... excuse me Ayesha, but I need your top."

The Caliph's daughter squeaked in surprise as he tore the flimsy covering from her. She turned the blade she was carrying on the sailor, but he backed away knotting the bloodied purple cloth round his knuckles. "You see what I'm doing?" he asked urgently.

"Living dangerously," the princess replied, understanding but glaring. "The Rakshasa should never have spilled my blood before I lost his game."

"Right. So if you've got to be cursed, at least let's make some use of it!" Sinbad sheathed his sword and went in with his fists. He somersaulted above Bakasur's twin blade swipe, and twin blade swipes landed on the Rakshasa's shoulders, and delivered an ear-boxing that made the monster's helmet clang.

It had much more effect on an armored giant half-tiger than it should have done. Bakasur shrieked, tossed Sinbad away, and clutched his head.

Sinbad landed lithely, rolled back in low, came up inside the staggering demon's guard, and delivered a one-two gut punch. Ornate armor dented beneath his fists.

"Again!" demanded Ayesha. "For all those he murdered before my eyes! Hit him again!"

Sinbad was almost distracted by the blouseless beauty dancing nearby cheering him on. He took the vision for inspiration instead, slamming blow after blow into the staggering Rakshasa.

Every hit burned away more of the creature's illusion, shattering armor, searing away fur, tearing into the creature's very substance. The Rakshasa fought back, dropping his blades to rely upon his claws, raking the sailor's torso and arms.

Sinbad battled on. The gauze rags on his fists shredded. The Rakshasa smiled a disconcerting feral-toothed grin of final triumph. Without those curse-bloodies scraps the hero could do no harm. "Run out of tricks, traveler? Oh dear."

Ayesha circled behind the Rakshasa. She'd torn off her veil and smeared it with her blood. She knotted it like a garrote around the monster's throat.

The Rakshasa swatted her away; a mistake, as the curse crippled him once more. Sinbad caught the wrapped purple linen and tightened it further around Bakasur's neck. He held on with all his strength as the injured demon struggled.

He realized that it might not be enough.

Ayesha called out once more. "Bold Sinbad…*duck!*"

The sailor released his hold on the Rakshasa. Ayesha swung Sinbad's scimitar, a scimitar newly slicked from her seeping wounds, and sliced cleanly through the Rakshasa's neck. Bakasur was already falling into rotting meat before he hit the floor and burst in a maggoty puddle.

Sinbad and Ayesha caught their breath.

"Well," the sailor said at last, "thank you for a very stimulating chess match."

The princess courtesyed as if she was at an emperor's court. "Thank you for a diverting afternoon. I believe that when you open those doors the last glamor will be broken. You will find yourself back on your ship with your crew, sailing to Tarshish."

"And you with us? I need to get you home."

Ayesha hesitated. "I don't think so. You've seen how powerful is the curse laid upon me. I don't know where I will end up, but it won't be your *Blue Nymph*. Nowhere pleasant, I expect."

The princess' naked face was even more lovely. Brave, sad, but unbowed, she was spectacular. "You're mine now," Sinbad reminded her. "I'll free you, of course."

"I don't think that's allowed," Ayesha suspected. "I suspect things will work against that. Still, if you happen across me as you wander on your adventures, perhaps you might rescue me again…master?"

Sinbad wanted to kiss her; but as a free woman. "I'll keep an eye out," he promised. "Maybe ask Geber the Wise, or any of the other spooky people I keep bumping into. Maybe your father might have some ideas if he decides not to behead me."

The tower of bone began to crumble. Some of the spine staircase collapsed.

"Our sands have run out, bold Sinbad," Ayesha declared.

"Until the glass turns again," the hero replied. "I told you, I usually get what I seek."

"Until that time, then. Good sailing, Sinbad the Sailor."

Ayesha opened the exit door. A blinding light enveloped them.

Sinbad opened his eyes on the deck of the *Blue Nymph*.

"What in heaven and all the hells just happened?" demanded Omar al-Keenjahar, Sinbad's first mate.

The sailor looked across the water at approaching Lanka. "Oh, a tiger and a lady, a door and a choice. Usual sort of thing," he answered flippantly as his gallant crew came to their senses.

Then his smile grew pensive and his eyes found the distance. "A most unusual sort of lady, though," he confessed.

In his hands he held Ayesha's veil, promise of another turn of the glass.

THE END

find the Lady

I consider it bad manners to leave a lady in a difficult predicament. I wasn't brought up that way.

So when I wrote "Sinbad and the Sapphire of the Djinn", my award-nominated story for *Sinbad: the New Voyages* volume 1, I was left with a dilemma. I'd established that the fair Princess Ayesha was kidnapped and spirited away, but that story wasn't about her. Sinbad took care of business, as a hero should, but by the end of that tale he'd never even *met* the girl.

In my mind she was still out there, still in distress, still in need of a bold swashbuckling sailor. Then Ron Fortier, editor-in-chief and captain of Airship 27, appealed for a short piece that would round out a fourth volume of Sinbad travels; and it occurred to me that perhaps this might be the time to offer Ayesha some aid.

Rakshasas are some of the most interesting and neglected monsters of myth. They originate from the Indian Hindu tradition, then worm their way into the Buddhist texts.[6] They are Asuras, semi-divine beings who have fallen, not unlike demons of Christian tradition who were once angels. In some ways they are the recurring enemies of the gods, as the frost giants were to the Norse deities of Asgard and the Formorians to the Irish Tuatha de Dannan; monstrous, powerful, magical, and predatory.

Rukh Bakasur takes his name from the Mahabharata, where his namesake terrorised the kingdom of Ekachakra into offering sacrifices to him, daily provisions for him to devour along with those who delivered them. He was slain by Bhima, second of the Pandava brothers. Bakasaur means "duck spirit" but I found no means of incorporating that into the story in this volume.

Taprobana or Taprobane is the Greek name for—probably—the island now called Sri Lanka, and it appeared as such on maps well into the seventeenth century. The Arabs called the island Serendib, the Fortunate Chance Isle, from whence comes our term serendipity. Ceylon was long held to be the ancestral stronghold of the Rakshasas.

Chess made its way from the Arabs to India, from thence to the Persian Empire, and so across the globe. Along the way it evolved and changed, as footnoted, but for the purposes of our present narrative I have assumed that a modern variant already existed at the time Sinbad encountered Aye-

---

6   They make their mark in the Hindu *Ramayana* and the *Mahabharata* and in the Buddhist *Theravada* and *Mahayana* literature.

sha. Bakasur's Taprobane is not entirely of this world, after all, and if he wishes to implement rules not common to the game until the eighteenth century, such as castling and the two-square pawn move, who is to argue with a seven-foot tiger-headed ravager?

Astute chess players may have noted that our game perfectly predicts the landmark strategies of Alexander Petrov in his 1844 Warsaw match with F. Alexander Hoffman, the centre attack game with queen sacrifice known as "Petrov's Immortal". For those who follow such detail, the game played then, and earlier as we now know by Sinbad and the maiden, runs as follows:

1. e4 e5 2. Nf3 Nc6 3. Bc4 Bc5 4. c3 Nf6 5. d4 ed4 6. e5 Ne4 7. Bd5 Nf2 8. Kf2 dc3 9. Kg3 cb2 10. Bb2 Ne7 11. Ng5 Nd5 12. Nf7 O-O 13. Nd8 Bf2 14. Kh3 d6 15. e6 Nf4 16. Kg4 Ne6 17. Ne6 Be6 18. Kg5 Rf5 19. Kg4 h5 20. Kh3 Rf3#

Rakshasas have a habit of not only carrying off young women but also of gambling for them. Like the tiger-headed creatures they sometimes choose to resemble (other times they appear as elephant-headed, multi-headed, multi-limbed, and in all kinds of weird shapes), the demons like to play with their prey.

Of course, a very short fill-in story to complete the word count of an anthology volume could not be sufficient to properly rescue so important a heroine as the Caliph of Baghdad's daughter. Haroun al Rashid's beautiful heiress is not so easily won. It may be that there is more to tell about the encounters of the world's most swashbuckling sailor and his age's most dazzling princess. Who knows which way the winds may blow?

I.A. WATSON-really likes his legends. As well as contributing to SINBAD: THE NEW VOYAGES volume 1 he has also provided Airship 27 with the novels ROBIN HOOD: KING OF SHERWOOD, ROBIN HOOD: ARROW OF JUSTICE, ROBIN HOOD: FREEDOM'S OUTLAW, and ROBIN HOOD: FORBIDDEN LEGEND, and with stories for the ongoing SHERLOCK HOLMES: CONSULTING DETECTIVE anthologies (six to date). Most of those stories have been nominated for awards; some even won them. His love of myth and the fabric of storytelling also manifests in his non-fiction essay collection WHERE STORIES DWELL, which even includes discussion of one of the world's first whodunits from Arabian Nights.

His other recent works include the "weird science" novels SIR MUMPHREY WILTON AND THE LOST CITY OF MYSTERY and THE TRANSDIMENSIONAL TRAVEL AGENCY, the e-novella fantasy series BYZANTIUM, and stories in the anthologies PRIDE OF THE MOHICANS and THE MANY WORLDS OF ULYSSES KING. His list of published works is now too long to include in a brief "about the author" section but a comprehensive list, along with free stories and background material, is available via http://www.chillwater.org.uk/writing/iawatsonhome.htm

I.A. Watson hopes to be remembered as a mythological bogeyman and a warning to children.

SET SAIL FOR ADVENTURE

The greatest seafaring adventurer of all times returns to the high seas, Sinbad the Sailor!

Born of countless legends and myths, this fearless rogue sets sail across the seven seas aboard his ship, the Blue Nymph, accompanied by an international crew of colorful, larger-than-life characters. Chief among these are the irascible Omar, a veteran seamen and trusted first mate, the blond Viking giant, Ralf Gunarson, the sophisticated archer from Gaul, Henri Delacrois and the mysterious, lovely and deadly female samurai, Tishimi Osara. All of them banded together to follow their famous captain on perilous new voyages across the world's oceans.

So pack up your you traveling bags, bid ado to your loved ones and get ready to sail with the tide as Sinbad El Ari takes the tiller and the Blue Nymph sets sails once more; its destination worlds of wonder, mystery and high adventure.

www.ingramcontent.com/pod-product-compliance
Lightning Source LLC
Chambersburg PA
CBHW071241250626
47163CB00001B/272